CRACH FFINNANT
RAVENS AND DRAGONS

VOLUME THREE

CRACH FFINNANT
RAVENS AND DRAGONS

Lazarus Carpenter

WORDS MATTER
P U B L I S H I N G
OUR WORDS CHANGE THE WORLD

Words Matter Publishing
P.O. Box 531
Salem, Il 62881
www.wordsmatterpublishing.com

ISBN 13: 978-1-949809-62-6

Library of Congress Catalog Card Number: 2020937973

ACKNOWLEDGEMENTS

I would like to express my sincerest gratitude to **Debbie Eve** whose wonderful illustrations have created visual memories for readers of the characters and scenes from my novels. Her work and support with the manuscript also included typing, partnering editing and proofing. We spent many hours travelling around Wales visiting places of interest related to our work for inspiration. Thank you for a magical partnership in our work and lives together.

My publisher **Tammy Koelling, Words Matter Publishing** for having faith and commitment to us and our work, The Crach Ffinnant series. Tammy, in addition to publishing Crach Ffinnant, believes the series would make a grand movie and is working hard to make this happen. Thank you.

For linguistic interpretation of Welsh language and phonetic guide, sincere thanks to **Nia Jenkins**.

Dedication

In memory of Crach Ffinnant

VOLUME III
CRACH FFINNANT
RAVENS AND DRAGONS

CHAPTER ONE

Our journey from Sycharth was swift and there was no doubt Tan-y-Mynedd achieved the great distance in record time, despite changing winds hampering our flight on occasions and me hanging on between his enormous scaled shoulders for my very life. A bright moon illuminated our passage but the great dragon frequently used clouds to conceal us from prying eyes; old habits die hard in these perilous times and were perhaps essential for our survival. Tan-y-Mynedd the Fire-Dragon soared skilfully ever onwards. The ground below rose and dipped away again into a deep valley, shrouded by mountains on all sides. The darkness of night began to fade and dawn lingered in wait upon the horizon. The great dragon pulled back both wings, thrust out a proud armoured chest, extended four thick, muscular, scaled legs, flexed talons and swished his tail high. Expelling hot air from both nostrils in clouds of steam, he landed rather less than gracefully on the scree-covered mountainside. Scrambling down from between the safety of Tan-y-Mynedd's huge armoured shoulders, legs shaking like jelly clothing brawn, my feet touched solid ground again. We had arrived once more at the Great Council of Blue Stone.

I sat with my old reptilian friend, Tan-y-Mynedd, at the long oak table surrounded by ancient members and old friends of the Council. All were familiar to me from the last time I was summoned here, but some were absent. Of the three dragons that had still survived, it was only Tan-y-Mynedd who represented them today. Graig-y-Graig, who was the eldest of all the reptiles, had been ill for some time due to his increasing years. The old dragon dropped off to sleep a few months ago deep in the caverns of Dan-yr-Ogof, never to wake up again. One was still missing, a continued source of great concern for all. Fwynedd the Shepherd sat opposite me, having returned from his village where he had been assisting in the preparation of its defence against the English soldiers roaming the countryside. Carron perched on my shoulder, playfully pecking at my earring as usual.

A constant sound of falling water filled the air. This was 'the world below our world', a magical and mystical place. Voices bounced off the walls, ancient languages merged with each other to form musical sounds, resonating in haunting beauty. Silent shadows danced around the cave walls, aided by flickering flames ushering from huge candles burning here and there. The atmosphere here always reminded me of how the air feels just before a huge storm, full of power and energy. My old teachers, Llwyd ap Crachan Llwyd and Myrddin Goch ap Cwnwrig, sat shimmering in all their splendour, smiling

4

warmly at me. Math Fab Mathonwy, who was seated next to Fwynedd, played with his enormous white beard, twirling and twisting strands between slender translucent fingers. Deep in conversation with the Elven elder, he seemed to be nodding in agreement to words I could not hear. A rather short goblin skipped from here to there, filling goblets with sweet mead and, unlike as with my clumsy friend, Crow, ne'er a drop was spilt. Chatter echoed throughout the grand cathedral cavern as an air of excitement and trepidation mingled with sounds of falling water.

Tree-Man shook his enormous ancient branches and the Eagle, pushing out a proud chest and fluttering huge wings, prepared to call the Council to order. A dwarf lifted the grand horn and breathing in the deepest of breaths, he placed it on waiting lips. Closing his eyes tightly, cheeks bulging full of air, the dwarf blew three times and Eagle fluttered his wings again.

***

"We will now move as does the wolf. We will be cautious, cunning, wise, and use our mountains and valleys as weapons against our enemies. Like the wolf, we will leave the bones of our enemies to bleach on the ground where they fall."

Words spoken by his brother Owain's speech from the proclamation at Sycharth echoed deep inside Tudur's mind. He, together with thirty soldiers, lay in wait for the sun to rise, armed to the teeth with axes, swords and spears, they secreted themselves in bushes and hollows within spitting distance of Ruthin. Nobody, nor anything, moved—all was silent. The English soldiers in the garrison slept soundly, even the guards must have felt safe as they too chased their dreams; perhaps the quaffing of ale hours previously had taken a toll. Either way, all was quiet.

A flash of sunlight streamed momentarily, heralding dawn. Tudur raised an arm in preparation for the signal to attack. He had decided to permanently silence the guards in their slumbers during the first sweep, whilst locking the gates to the garrison behind them. They would then disable the English soldiers by whatever means necessary, but it seemed unlikely many would be spared the sword. Tempers were running very high, but the focus of Tudur and his men upon the task given to them by his brother, Owain Glyndwr, Prince of Wales, remained uppermost in their minds.

A dog fox barked in the distance as dawn broke in cloudy fragments across the early morning sky. All eyes fell upon Tudur's arm and as the cock crowed, down it came and up he sprang, accompanied by his men. Silently and with great haste and skill, Tudur's men crept up behind each guard and waited. A thwarted impression of an owl hoot echoed and all sprang at once upon their prey, daggers seeking jugulars. Guards, now dead and unable to warn anybody again, lay prostrate where they had been slain by their silent assassins. They were a stark reminder of the burning wrath now held by the Welsh against the English. Each Welsh soldier crept quietly into the garrison through the now unguarded gate or stealthily climbed over the once guarded walls. With the gate locked behind them, Tudur and his men stormed into the barn where all those asleep were soon to be slaughtered. An English soldier woke with a start, but quickly returned to sleep when Emrys smashed him in the face with a hammer.

Tudur's men fell on the sleeping and drowsy soldiers; stabbing, slashing and cutting each where they lay. As quickly as it started, all was over.

Tudur wiped a bloody sword blade across a blanket and turning to his men, whispered.

"Where are their officers? Find them."

Three of the Welsh soldiers quietly searched elsewhere for any English they may have missed. Tudur whispered again.

"We have the garrison, Ruthin is ours and the town's folk will know it."

He turned towards Emrys and grimaced before spitting his words.

"Wake them all and gather them in the square, separate the Welsh from the English! Ruthin will see justice this day."

The morning sun struggled to shine through a cloud-driven sky and rain hung in the air in silent wait, preparing to soak the earth below. All the villagers rousted from warm beds, gathered in the square and, as instructed, Emrys and his men split them up into two groups, English and Welsh. Protestations from some left Emrys in no doubt there were English, pretending to be otherwise, but they soon sorted the wheat from the chaff.

*****

Crow, as usual, was sprawled on hands and knees, slipping and sliding as he tried to regain balance, which proved a little difficult with so many baby dragons jumping all over him. They really did enjoy nipping him with those sharp, tiny, needle-like teeth and chasing poor Crow was their only fixation in life at the moment. Faerydae laughed as she tried to help him gather them up but it was just a little difficult, if not impossible. The young dragons had started to realise their tiny wings did a little more than simply flap. Perching on top of the nest, they leapt off and with every little flutter and flap, found they could stay in the air a little longer; flight was not far away. Crow knew this, and so did Faerydae. The trials and tribulations of the 'now' paled in comparison to the future when seventeen baby dragons would take to the wing and that would make life in the nursery somewhat difficult! It was hard enough to keep them safe at the moment but once they could fly, all sorts of things may go wrong and with such precious dragon babies as these, who were crucial to the survival of the species, all care that could be taken, must be taken. Crow trembled with anxiety at the mere thought of anything happening to his charges.

CHAPTER TWO

I sat leaning against an enormous aged and gnarled tree trunk. The air was chilled and I shivered, pulling the sheepskin coat tight around my small frame, its collar sheltering my ears which were being insulted by a harsh wind gusting from the north. Fortunately, my trousers were thick and warm and my boots were dry over thick socks. My beard somewhat protected my face and the coat's hood, my head, but my nose, well that was another story. Protruding as it did, the word cold is an understatement and you must believe me when I say, blue and purple replaced its usual pink.

I felt very tired after walking so far over three days and with very little sleep to speak of. Merlina, my faithful old pony, carried my few needs of a bed roll and food. Her load was enough so I did not ride her. The ageing mare had served me well and she was nearly thirty years old now. As I journeyed to Ffestiniog, my intention was to bring back the warhorse who was currently in the care of my old friend, Crow. Merlina stood silently, tethered to a tree behind me, tail flicking, head deep inside a nose bag of corn. My mind wandered as I became physically warmer, tired eyelids fluttered and I could feel sleep falling over me like a velvet cloak. Staring at the mountainside in front of me, eyelids getting heavier as my vision became hazy, sleep was only moments away.

***

Behind a large table, ensconced in a most comfortable chair, sat King Henry with a goblet of wine in one hand and a dagger in the other, toying its point on the table as his thoughts drifted to his army of ten thousand troops who were camped just beyond Chester on a march to Scotland. Lord Edmund sat to one side of Henry, looking none the worse for his encounter with Glyndwr and the failed ransom attempt some months ago. Now in the finery of a Lord and Knight, he looked the part with ruffs and breastplate, fine leather thigh riding boots and cloak with delicate embroidery. This peacock of a man was all mouth with little bravery unless hidden by the skirts of the King. Sat next to him, Lord Essex fiddled with a leg of chicken, staring intently at the departed fowl, he then sniffed at it, curling his nose in disgust.

"Something wrong with your food, Essex?" Henry leaned forward, pointing the dagger to emphasise his question.

"This foul is rank!" Essex remarked.

"We are at war, man!" the King hurled his words menacingly across the table. "I have eaten it and so has Edmund. Have you not, Edmund?"

Lord Essex breathed a sigh of relief as Henry turned

his attentions towards Edmund. Edmund had not so much as nibbled at the chicken, his delicate constitution silently informing him to leave well alone. Edmund looked at the ground, unable to face the King.

"So, Edmund the food at your King's table is not good enough for you either?" Henry's voice rose a few notches with obvious irritation at Edmund who was now adding to his already foul temper. Just as the King swiped his goblet off the table, a soldier opened a tent flap, allowing a gust of cold air to usher forth, fanning the flames which burst from embers in the brazier warming them.

"My King!" the soldier shouted bending his head in respect. "A messenger from Wales awaits your pleasure."

"Ah!" Henry's temper subsided and a wry smile crept across his face. "One of your spies, Essex?" he questioned, while not requiring an answer. "Send him in!" Henry supported his words with a wave of a hand, still holding the dagger between his fingers.

The soldier walked backwards from the tent. As the tent flap re-opened, the brazier coals again flickered into flame as a further gust of freezing air fanned them. In no time at all the tent flap widened, held open by a soldier, enabling the messenger to enter.

"Shut the flap, man!" Henry shouted. "Come!" He beckoned to the messenger a silent 'step forward'. He then turned towards Essex, all thoughts of the chicken now past. "Is this your man, Essex?"

Essex replied. "Yes, my Lord, it is." He turned to face the messenger. "You have news, man?"

"I do sir!" The messenger bowed slowly.

"Enough of that!" Henry shouted. "Get on with it!"

The messenger, dressed in riding leathers, was soaked

to the skin from rain and his cloak, like his breeches, were splattered with mud from hard riding. Bedraggled wet hair hung in ringlets to broad shoulders. Two daggers held in a belt were criss-crossed over his middle and a sword hung from a scabbard at his side. His features were sharp, his skin chiselled with pox scars and his chin sprouted a whispery beard. "I come from Ruthin, my Lord, riding like the wind. I have grave news and poor tidings to come!"

"Get on with it, man!" Henry spurred him on, intrigued to hear what was so important to disturb his royal repast.

"My King, Glyndwr's men have stormed Ruthin. The garrison is taken and they have executed those of our men who did not fall to the sword. The town is captured and put to the torch, my Lord." He bowed with as much grace as his appearance could muster.

Henry flew into a rage. He stood up, crashing both fists into the table.

"My Lord, p...p...pray there is more!" The messenger stumbled over his words.

Both Essex and Edmund pushed their chairs in reverse, attempting to avoid the King's wrath which was about to explode like a volcano. Essex leaned forward, interjecting firmly. "The rest of the news, if you please?"

The King sat down, glaring at the bedraggled messenger. "Yes, yes get on with it!" Henry added, less angry but no less irritated by the news heard thus far.

"Sir, he was proclaimed Prince!" the messenger said.

"Prince!" Henry was beginning to become furious.

The messenger continued, "After the proclamation, his men attacked Ruthin, Denbigh, Rhuddlan, Flint, Hawarden and Holt. They have all fallen, sir. Ruthin is burned to the ground, only the castle and Nantclwyd y Dre still stands.

They were moving on Oswestry, Sir, as I rode north with this news."

Henry was speechless, he simply sat staring at the ceiling of the tent, his face drained, and eyes seemingly empty and blank. Essex broke the silence, asking the messenger if that was all the news he had to give. The messenger seemed uneasy, moving from foot to foot anxiously. He coughed, rubbed spittle from his chin with a dirty gloved hand and stared passed the King, looking over the royal shoulder. It was forbidden for the common man to look directly at a royal personage. The anxious messenger continued.

"My Lord, by now they will have struck on Oswestry, but I know not the outcome at this time." He coughed again. "There is something else!"

"Something else?" interjected Henry, somewhat angrily, though possibly understandable under the circumstances. "What is it?"

"Dragons, My Lord!" shrieked the messenger shuffling on the spot where he stood.

"Dragons!" the King, Essex and Edmund all exclaimed in unison, turning to look at each other, somewhat shocked at hearing the word, 'dragons'.

The messenger went on to explain, "I was passing through a village in the North at the border and stopped to water my horse and eat a crust. I overheard a shepherd and a dwarf talking in a hostelry. They were almost whispering to each other and when I thought I heard the word 'dragon', I listened carefully and attempted to catch as much as I could, given their quiet conversation. I could not hear all, but I heard of eggs and young dragons. I also heard the name, Tan-y-Mynedd." He paused.

"I have heard that name before." Henry looked at

Edmund. "That is the dragon Erasmus spoke of. Where is that old wizard?"

Henry Bolingbroke, King of England, sat and schemed. Within minutes, he ordered the messenger to go and eat, then ride to London.

"Go to the Lord of Leicester and tell him to despatch a troop to find Erasmus, leaving no stone unturned." He paused and drank wine from his goblet. "Essex, inform the captains to turn the army and prepare for battle. When the cock crows, we march on Wales and Glyndwr's traitorous army of serfs!" He turned to face Edmund. "You, Sir, will take two men and find out if the story of the dragons is true."

Edmund shuffled uneasily in his chair. "What do you want me to do if it is true, my Lord?"

"Kill or capture, Edmund, kill or capture! I charge you to put an end to this one way or another." The King pointed his dagger towards Edmund. "Do not fail me again, Edmund, or next time, I will have your head. Do you understand?" Edmund glanced around for support from Essex, but none came. "Now, Edmund! Not in the morning - now!" Henry stabbed the dagger into the table.

***

When I awoke from my slumbers, I recalled a vivid dream in which King Henry had learnt of the young dragons. As my dreams are always prophetic, I decided my journey to Ffestiniog was now most urgent and I set out at a pace three times that of my usual strolling gait. A sturdy staff gave me an extra foothold on sliding scree, damp and greasy from the earlier rain, making it even more treacherous than when dry. I went down into the valley, traversing a fierce outcrop of rock while avoiding a sheer drop, and continued my descent.

Rain hung in the sky, threatening a downpour but a threat is all it turned out to be. In the distance, a weary sun tried to warm this day, but failed miserably when being hidden, once more, by masses of encroaching grey rain-laden clouds. Whilst walking quickly, well as much as it was possible for my small legs to achieve, especially when foothold and grip are as precarious as that below my feet, creating added anxiety to the words I had heard and the scene I had witnessed in my dreamscape. Sadly, an eavesdropper in the service of the King had overheard a dwarf and a tall elderly shepherd whispering about dragons. This was most unfortunate and it is clear from the descriptions given it was Crow and Fwynedd who had innocently committed the gravest of errors.

CHAPTER THREE

An argument ensued in a tent nearby to the King's. Not as yet having embarked on the missions given them by Henry, Lord Essex fumed at Edmund.

"You are a churl, Sir! And, believe me, my words, are the kindest you will hear from me upon this day."

Lord Essex had never liked Edmund and the events of recent months did naught to sway his opinion.

"If the King had no need of such a lap dog as you, Edmund, my life would be sweeter. You have no backbone, Sir, and no opinions worthy of support. Never have I met another so devoid of charity for his fellows. And yet, you are the first to moan when all is not to your liking, the first to cry when pain is merely due to a scratch on life's pathways. You lack the ability to use sound judgement when the occasion demands, are the first to blame others when the fault often lays at your own feet. Why, Sir—why do you have so much luck? The fact Glyndwr let you live is a decision I will never understand. Perhaps it was that damn dwarf again, interceding on your behalf, thus enabling your feud of decades to continue? Or, perhaps not?"

Edmund stood as Essex pulled back the tent flap to leave.

"My Lord Essex, I do not wish to argue with you but I am offended by your words and the King shall hear of this. I am commanded to seek the dragon, a task riddled with unknown peril and you, Sir, berate me thus!"

Edmund rarely stood his ground but the importance of this new mission had inflated his already huge ego.

Essex dropped the tent flap, turning on Edmund fiercely.

"You are offended by my words and yet these are also the same words your King has uttered to you countless times. Are you deaf, or are you devoid of any intellect?"

Essex stepped towards Edmund, his fist raised in anger and frustration. Instinctively Edmund stepped back three paces, his right hand moving to grip his sword. Essex saw Edmund's move but his reaction was much swifter and his own sword left its scabbard in a flash, with a menacing point arriving at Edmund's throat.

"Stand down, Sir!" Essex commanded. "If your sword moves more, I will spike you like a chicken!"

Edmund's hand fell to his side. His face the colour of an evening sunset, pulses in his neck visibly throbbing, blood boiling. Edmund barked "I demand satisfaction, Essex, your insults and actions go too far!"

Essex laughed genuinely, with no scorn in his guffaw. "Every word I speak is the truth, go tell the King, I care not!" He continued to laugh and then suddenly, all mirth left his face. "Believe me when I say the satisfaction you have this night Edmund, is that you still breathe!"

Essex returned his sword, sheathing the blade safely in the scabbard hanging from his belt. His left hand hovered over the hilt of a dagger on his mid-drift. He did not trust Edmund as far as he could flick a flea. Cowardice was one of Edmund's most notable qualities. Essex was a far too shrewd and experienced battle-weary knight to ever fall to a ploy by Edmund. But Edmund also knew when to back off from a fight he was certain to lose. After all, only a coward and a bully will fight a lesser man. At head and shoulders twice above Edmund and each shoulder as wide, this battle-hardy warrior was not one Edmund should quarrel with.

"Very well, Essex. I accept your apology and will say no more, Sir!"

Essex stood perplexed, wishing he had not just heard the words he had. Still, surprised, he was not. Edmund was so adept at changing sides on a whim, his ability to appear to surrender, yet not, whilst projecting blame upon others, never accepting responsibility, was his way. Momentarily, Essex pondered and for a fraction of a second considered finishing the matter here and now. 'Raven's breath to the consequences', crossed his mind, but common sense reigned a balanced judgement, thus he answered Lord Edmund.

"As my Lord suggests!" Essex sarcastically glared at Edmund and if looks could kill—well, the rest is up to your imagination!

"I do accept your apology—I do!" Edmund added.

"I am sure that is so, Edmund. I have no more time to waste here. We both have our commands. I will rise to mine and I suggest you do the same, Sir, but beware the dragon's flame, Edmund, please try to avoid all fire-belching breath.

I would hate to see you with a scorched backside—but then perhaps not, eh?" Essex laughed heartily, with a hint of sarcasm in his voice. Flipping back the tent flap, he was gone.

Edmund stared at the empty space and heaved a sigh of genuine relief. His mouth had nearly got him killed—yet again. Even Edmund was not completely stupid enough to think he would stand an earthly chance in a battle with a warrior such as Essex. He would be a fool to consider such. Edmund sat down and stared towards the roof of the tent, a stain on the canvas drew a concentrated gaze which blurred into a deeper dreamlike state. Edmund's mind drifted.

CHAPTER FOUR

The ability to see and hear, let alone travel through time, are clearly most advantageous to this dwarf, as I am certain it would be to any sentient being. The fact I could perceive and see things others could not, aided my work with Owain in the most magical of ways, I jest with you not.

Let me digress and share a story from my dim and distant past, some ten years or more ago. A lesson to be learned for all, but for me, it was a hard place to be. We are all 'the masters of our own fate'.

***

Septimus Tupp was a monk in Valle Crucis Abbey where I would frequently see him on my visits to the Abbot, who was a friend of mine. Septimus was a difficult man and sadly most unsuccessful at practically everything he put his hand to. Perhaps the Gods had dealt him the most difficult of paths or perhaps he had chosen his own path by ignoring blatant lessons to enable success. Septimus Tupp would never learn. It is worthy to note that in the Welsh language, the word 'Tupp' implies a certain lacking of intellect, a dimness of mind perchance. I am being kind in my definition! Septimus Tupp lived up to his name.

It was a sunny July morning in 1390 when I arrived at the Abbey after a long hot and sweaty ride from Sycharth, stopping off at the blacksmith's in Llangollen after Merlina had thrown a shoe. I could never truly understand why we put iron shoes on horses' hooves. Surely all hooves must wear down and nailing iron just did not make sense to this dwarf. I mused upon this while Merlina was under the blacksmith's pedicure and came to the conclusion that maybe the hoof might wear too low. Anyway, Merlina was certainly not keen on the experience at the blacksmith's hands, of this, there was no doubt. Who could blame her when there she stands whilst a giant of a man such as Bryn Gwyn hammers nails into her toes! Merlina is a pony like many, blessed with expression and emotion oozing from her eyes but on this occasion, emotion turned to a physical assault on poor old Bryn. With shoeing complete, she nipped his large bottom as he walked past. It certainly made him jump! I am sure Merlina was smiling as her teeth met flesh. For a mountain of a man, Bryn Gwyn could jump quite high, well certainly much higher than he expected to! But Bryn was a gentle giant and even in shock and pain, he turned and softly stroked Merlina's nose.

"You got me a good one there, old girl!" he chuckled. "Happens all the time but still makes me jump," he added.

When I shared my thoughts about hooves and iron nails,

he told me the shoes prevented the walls of the hoof from wearing down or deforming in growth. Whilst I have no problem in understanding the ethos behind such a practice, it is the nailing of feet which makes me squirm, but Bryn told me the hoof wall is numb to any pain where the nails are hammered in. "Tell that to Merlina and your bruised bottom!" I laughed.

But back to Septimus Tupp! Upon my arrival at Valle Crucis Abbey, I saw his enormous bulk, sitting ensconced on a bench in the garden with plump fingers wrapped around an apple, half of which disappeared in one bite, consumed by an ever-hungry mouth. Drool dripped from an over-ripe jowl as he seemed to have no wish to chew and I believe he swallowed the huge chunk whole. His neck was so large, it was impossible to discern. Rolls of fat met with each other, as do the mountains with the valleys, merging to confuse any onlooker. Man or mountain was a question many asked when regarding Septimus Tupp. Adding such self-indulgence to a rather stilted intellect, Septimus was probably one of the most difficult of people I had ever encountered, even to this day. He was not a popular monk at the Abbey and most considered that Septimus believed all the other monks were at his beck and call, especially those who toiled in the kitchens! His own job at the Abbey used to be as an illustrator of their holy books, however, his plump fingers had been unable to grasp at a quill or brush for many a year. These plump fingers could no longer manage the delicate work needed. His belly was now so rotund, even getting close enough to a desk was impossible. All this, added to his constant drooling upon any work he might create, meant Septimus did little except eat enough for at least three men, as well as drain the wine caskets from the cellars. To say he was tolerated at the Abbey is no understatement. On every visit I made, he was always in someone's disfavour. My current visit proved to be no exception to this now well accustomed fact.

As I walked towards Septimus Tupp, he appeared to cough and his face became purple and red, just like a beetroot. Upon nearing the bench where he sat, I could clearly see he must have a piece of apple wedged in his fat gullet. On realising the danger this could cause, I quickly ran to him and without further ado, smacked him firmly in the middle of his extremely broad back. Septimus Tupp coughed with the bark of a dragon, paused momentarily to gasp for air, yet to be forthcoming, when up came the best part of half of the apple. Just as I suspected, his greed had yet again almost been the end of him. I stood back as he balked and choked in an attempt to regain breath to his enormous bulk.

"Hold hard, Dwarf!" Septimus shouted between gasps while dealing with the sharp blow I previously administered to his back. "That hurt! It stings—it stings!"

'*No thanks here then*', I mused as Septimus picked up the hitherto rejected apple from the floor and proceeded to bite it in half. Perhaps he may consider chewing it this time, or perhaps not.

He looked at me with his two piggy-like eyes peering through heavily over-burdened cheeks from under a precipice of a forehead and questioned. "Did you have to hit me so hard?" He tried to reach to where I had slapped him, to enforce his point, but chubby fingers could not touch where his arms could not reach. "You dwarfs just do not realise your own strength, do you?"

I did not think his comment deserved the consideration of a reply as I probably just saved his life, something that

Septimus Tupp overlooked in his eagerness to return to the apple!

"Dear Septimus Tupp," I said. "It is most fortunate I happened along at this time, otherwise you may now be but a heap on the ground, waiting to enter your Lord's Kingdom, no doubt!"

If I sounded sarcastic, I have no apology as I meant to be. This man even wears my patience to a veritable end.

"I was swallowing, when it just got a little bit stuck!" he blurted.

"You were choking, Septimus!" I retorted.

"If you say so, Dwarf. If you say so!" Septimus said as he placed the other half of the apple towards his mouth, although I did not see his mouth open as such, it simply merged with the jowl and then seemed as if his face was in the midst of an earthquake!

"So, you are well now, Septimus?" I smiled as much as my conscience would allow. "I must be about my business. Do you know where I may find the Abbot?"

Septimus Tupp raised a large arm and pointing a plump finger towards the lake, he spluttered. "By the lake." Bits of apple flew here and there, between each word. "Counting the fish, I expect!" he added.

I raised my hand in a partial gesture of farewell to Septimus Tupp and meandered in the direction of the lake where I soon saw the Abbot staring into the water.

As I approached, the reflections of oak and sycamore trees that surrounded the lakeside mirrored across its surface, and the sun-twinkled beams bounced from the ripples. Fish jumped here and there. This was a very well-stocked lake and fed the monks and their many visitors extremely well.

The Abbot turned as I was almost upon him and I saw him smile at seeing me. We had known each other for many years now.

"Crach Ffinnant, my dear friend. What a pleasure it is to see you!" the Abbot exclaimed as he started to walk towards me with his arms outstretched in greeting. "To what do I owe this visit, Crach?"

I had brought some letters from Owain who wanted the Abbot's advice on property boundaries.

"I bring questions for you from The Squire of Glyndwfry," I replied as we grasped each other's forearms in welcome before we hugged warmly. Although I am a dwarf, the Abbot was quite a short man in stature so it was not the usual struggle I might expect when greeting another!

"I see Septimus is 'as ever'," I said, smiling, but with some concern in my words. Although I was not too fond of him, or of myself for that matter at feeling like this about the fat monk. I really should have more patience with him but I do not seem to be able to find any. Even dwarfs are not perfect though, well certainly not this one but I do try to have charity for others, believe you me, and I have given Septimus Tupp so much rope of opportunity, he has hung himself several times over!

"Yes! I am afraid he grows more self-indulgent by the day, consuming enough food for three men. You see, he contributes little as it is, and he lacks the ability to complete the most menial of tasks." The Abbot looked perplexed. "We must care for our sick, it is our way. But, Crach, I ask you, is he sick?"

"If you are asking me if self-indulgence is a sickness, it must be if he lacks control."

"But, Crach!" The Abbot rubbed his hands together and

dug his feet into the earth. "It is a sin to indulge so, thus he transgresses every rule of our code."

"Then you do have a problem, my friend!" I replied.

Often the Abbot and I enjoyed our discussions about ecclesiastical matters. Although I did not share his religious persuasions, I saw some meanings in his teachings. My ways were about the earth and the sun, the moon and all life in nature. Nature gives us all we need, including prophecy. I like the stories he told me from his big book which he called the Bible but, to me, my way was a belief in a natural life, moving and changing with the seasons, listening to nature and living within it and all there is to enjoy.

"I don't know what to do with him." The Abbot gesticulated confusion, raising his shoulders in resignation. "I can't send him away and I have no idea as to how to resolve this, Crach. No idea!"

"Is there any job he can do, my Lord Abbot?" I asked.

"No, Crach, none. We have tried him with everything—and I do mean everything," he replied.

"Well, no doubt nature will take its course," I suggested.

The Abbot, for all his compassion and understanding, for a brief moment, looked cross, if not furious. "Yes, but at what cost, Crach? At what cost?" Rising eyebrows heralded the return of his smile as he recovered from his recent lapse.

"At what cost?" I asked, returning his question.

He looked sad as the light briefly left his eyes again. "Money, I am afraid. As at the end of every day, no matter what I may think or who I may aspire to be, it does fall down to money. We are a busy Abbey, as you know, with many visitors and a number of lay monks to support, in addition to the brothers. No matter how many grains of seed I consider, you will agree there is a village of mouths to feed."

I nodded in agreement.

"And, Septimus," he continued. "He contributes little. He is not even slightly amusing so the attribute of 'a fool' is even denied him. I despair. I only hope God will give good grace in this matter as, indeed, we all must do."

"As I said earlier, nature must take its course," I responded.

There had been many times Septimus Tupp wished things could have been different but everything was so 'black and white', either it was or it was not. Poor Septimus, he had been a grand, skilled illustrator many years ago. He now sat on life's road in his fourth decade and, in my opinion, he was on the eve of his latter days. All his past glories, although factual, had been somewhat lost in the mists of time, replaced by gross self-indulgence and little to no ability to discern reason. It is sad to admit, but Septimus Tupp appeared a lost cause, merely a soul to pity. I knew my friend, the Abbot, felt the same way. I think he almost admitted as much during our recent nattering. How sad life can be.

The Abbot and I walked slowly on the loose gravel path. Chippings slipped between my sandals and toes making me smart with discomfort. With the lake behind us, we wandered on towards where Septimus sat, staring at the sky, eating yet another apple. A bright sun sparkled through the branches and leaves of a host of trees, it was such a beautiful day. Swallows swooped here and there, taking insects from low to the ground and soaring upwards for more. A thrush sang from a nearby bush, taking to the wing as we approached. As we drew closer to Septimus, he wobbled and struggled from the bench, managing to make it to his feet without major incident.

"My Lord Abbot." Septimus beckoned. "Good afternoon to you and greetings again to you, Crach Ffinnant."

I silently returned his greeting with a nod of my head and a wink of my eye.

"And to you, Brother Septimus—and to you." The Abbot returned his greeting.

The Abbot smiled and gesticulated a suggestion that Septimus may be better staying seated. He did not need telling twice and quickly returned, unceremoniously, to the bench with a thud.

"Thank you, My Lord Abbot. It is a hot day for standing around."

Beads of sweat rolled from the fat monk's forehead which he patted furiously with a stained rag.

"Are there sufficient fish?" Septimus questioned.

"What?" queried the Abbot, somewhat surprised.

"You counted the fish!" affirmed Septimus.

"Counted the fish?" the Abbot queried again, with even more surprise.

"He thinks you have been counting the fish in the lake," I interjected.

"What on earth for?" exclaimed the Abbot. "Why would I count the fish in the lake?"

"To make sure there is enough for dinner. I think you need to know that, don't you?" Septimus asked.

There was, of course, a simple logic to his question. Such is the way of Septimus. His black and white thinking makes him question that which others take for granted. But in his day, this simple monk was an artist of the best calibre, now he was an artist of food—eating it!

The Abbot clearly sensed his confusion and decided to go along with Septimus. Somehow, it just seemed the easiest way. "Yes, there are enough fish, Brother Septimus. Nobody will go hungry."

"Oh good!" Septimus was now drooling at the mere thought of fried fish. "Fish for tea! I will look forward to that, in fact, I would love that!" he exclaimed as he continued to drool.

"Brother Septimus." The Abbot looked straight into the monk's face. "We need to catch some fish from the lake first and I would like you to do that for me if you would be so kind?"

"I will," agreed Septimus. "I would be 'so kind', as I would love some lovely fish! Will I need to use a net?" he asked.

"You will, Septimus. The net is on the raft," the Abbot replied.

A flat raft was kept tethered by the lakeside and was an excellent vantage point to net fish. Even dear Septimus Tupp could catch fish from here.

"Is this a job he has done before?" I quietly asked the Abbot.

"Once or twice," he replied.

"Successfully?" I queried.

The Abbot merely shrugged his shoulders.

Septimus struggled to his feet and ambled slowly towards the lake, humming a tune only he knew.

The Abbot and I walked on, leaving the Abbey and its lake behind us. A little way along the valley stood a monument to the Great Kings of Powys and their ancient ancestors. To me, this was a place of pilgrimage whenever I visited the Abbey as fortunately, it stood only a fifteen-minute easy walk away. The Abbey Valle Crucis (Valley of the Cross) can thank the Pillar of Eliseg for its name. Eliseg was the great grandfather of King Concenn, who lived nearly seven hundred years ago. This monument was the very bloodline of Owain's ancestors and on my frequent visits to the Abbey, I would visit it and consider 'The Prophecy', believing that the dragon will rise again. So much of this knowledge is many years lost to most, but the sacred records held by the Council of Blue Stone remember all.

The Abbot stood gazing up at the valley cliffs and the rich forest adorning the earth like a tapestry. This was a sacred place in life and legend, a place to cherish and behold the ancient stories held by this stone.

"I will let you sit with your dreams of prophecy and princes, Crach. I will return to the Abbey and see you at dinner. Hopefully, we will be serving you fish!" We both laughed as he walked back on the path we had come.

I sat in silence by The Pillar of Eliseg. The Abbot was right, I did dream of prophecies and princes. I saw Glyndwr crowned Prince of Wales in years yet to come.

An evening sun took precedence in the sky and my tummy gurgled with hunger pangs, taking precedence on earth! It was time for me to return to the Abbey and, hopefully, Septimus may have netted some fish for our dinner. In anticipation, I could almost smell fried fish and even taste it too. I really hoped Brother Septimus had been successful in his task.

As I returned through the gates of the Abbey, I could hear a commotion. I saw monks scattering from their tasks, appearing to be frightened and confused.

"Fetch the Abbot!" I heard one shout. "Somebody, fetch the Abbot at once!"

A monk rushed past me and onwards towards the lake. I followed him to where I found several of the brothers stood staring at the water and something rather large floating on it.

"Oh, by dragon's breath," I mumbled to myself. It looked like Septimus, floating on the lake.

At that moment, the Abbot, together with two monks

ran past me.

"Get in there and get him out!" the Abbot commanded. "In the name of God, get him out of there!"

By the time I reached the edge of the lake, two monks had swum out to where Septimus Tupp floated face down and were attempting to pull him to shore. It would take more than two of them to lift him out at the shoreline that was certain. The monks in the lake were hampered by the extra weight of their baggy woollen habits, now sodden. However, they struggled on and were now knee-deep at the shoreline, but the enormous bulk of the soul, latterly known as Septimus Tupp, just stuck in the shallows, refusing to move. The thought came to me, '*as in life, so in death*', but it was an unkind thought and I dismissed it from my mind. Four other monks joined them, knee-deep in the lake. Two monks took a limb each, while the others supported the head and shoulders of Septimus Tupp. Between the six of them, they huffed and puffed, wheezed and coughed, spluttered and even swore under their breath. I am sure this is where the expression 'dead weight' originates. A body always seems heavier in death and for Septimus Tupp, this was certainly true. Finally, the six monks recovered the body to the grassy verge at the edge of the shoreline.

When the Prior shuffled up behind the Abbot, he was bending over Septimus and his lifeless form. The Prior was a scrawny little man, always giggling nervously as if he were in a constant state of surprise. He had a narrow forehead, shaded by the front of his tonsure and hooked nose like a falcon. A chin pointed and blotched by stubble, supported a tiny tight mouth with hardly any lips visible at all. He was wringing his hands and stepping nervously from foot to foot.

"What happened? Oh dear! Poor Septimus." The Prior continued to hop from one foot to the other and still, he wrung his hands, unable to stay still. "Is he dead?"

"I am afraid so," replied the Abbot. "He has clearly drowned but I fail to see why he ended up in the lake. Even at its deepest, it barely covers my head." He scratched his chin and looked down at Septimus with a puzzled glance, before calling to me. "Crach! Please come and take a look at Septimus."

"Yes, of course, Abbot," I replied and took a few steps to his side. Bending down on one knee, I slowly looked at the body, starting with his head. I saw no bruises, cuts or abrasions on his head or neck. In fact, there was not a mark on Septimus Tupp at all, other than the mark of gluttony I thought quietly to myself.

"I asked him to stand on the pontoon and catch some fish for our evening meal," the Abbot stated. "He must have fallen in by being over-balanced, judging by the sight of the net so heavily laden with fish."

I had to agree with his assumption but added, "Well if he fell headfirst, the chances are he would not have been able to right his posture or raise his head because of his excessive weight. He certainly would not have been able to use his arms to swim. An unfortunate accident, my Lord Abbot."

"Yes, indeed, Crach. But it fills me with sadness we should have been discussing him only this morning and in the way we did too—most uncharitable of me indeed—most uncharitable."

He made a very good point. I also felt pangs of conscience. After all, I too had not been particularly charitable to Septimus Tupp either. Sadly, he was as much a victim of his own gluttony in death as he was in life. A sad but totally inevitable outcome when we consider the man could hardly walk, yet we had considered he may swim with such bulk and restrictive movements. Although he would have died quite quickly, it was a very unfortunate accident and perhaps one that had been in waiting for some time.

"This is tragic, Crach," the Abbot interrupted my thoughts.

"What must we do now?" asked the Prior. "Oh dear." He was clearly agitated, his face screwed and contorted with morbid anxiety.

"Worry not, my good Prior. Let the lay brothers take him to the Abbey sickbay where last offices can be done. Now get along, and try not to fuss so," the Abbot advised.

The Prior gave a perfunctory nod of his head, black eyes darting from here to there as he scuttled off in the direction of the Abbey.

"Such a nervous little man," said the Abbot, speaking his thoughts out loud.

"Indeed, my Lord Abbot," I responded. "It seems the Prior is to anxiety as Septimus Tupp was to gluttony."

"We certainly have been taught some lessons in humility today, Crach," observed the Abbot.

I looked back over the lake and wondered if the ghost of Septimus Tupp might be seen there in years to come. We may never know.

CHAPTER FIVE

Travelling through the time portal to Ffestiniog was a little
less fraught this time, given the absence of a warhorse!
Unreal sensations of travelling at speed with a feeling of being
grounded and yet not, with images passing by to the left and
right of me when there, right in front, a black dot vibrating
and growing. I had arrived. My exit this time was a little more
dignified than the last, landing firmly on two feet with not a
scratch, contrary to the last journey. Although physically long
gone, my mind still smarted at the pain experienced when I
landed on the hard stone floor.

Making my way through the caverns towards the dragons'
lair, I could hear the familiar voices and laughter of Faerydae,
Crow and, if my ears were in good working order, I fancy I
heard Fwynedd. How fortunate for them all to be here at the

same time as we had grave tidings to discuss, given what now was known about Henry's orders to seek out the dragons to either tame or destroy.

"Crach!" Crow was the first to see me enter the cavern. "Everybody! Crach returns!"

Tan-y-Mynedd gave a swish of his huge tail and several baby dragons appeared. Two took to flight, whilst others scampered here and there. One landed from flight onto Crow's shoulder and playfully nipped his ear. Playfully, it may have been, but nonetheless painful for the ever-clumsy dwarf!

"Ouch! That hurt!" Crow protested.

Faerydae and Fwynedd laughed out loud and Tan-y-Mynedd sneezed, making everybody duck, except me! Off I flew through the air, skidding on my bottom along the hard cavern floor. They all laughed, the great dragon guffawed and I swear I heard the baby dragons giggling. My bottom was sore and a new graze appeared on my knee, reminding me I should not have counted my chickens, so to speak, when I exited the portal a little while ago.

"Well, Dwarf! I got you!" Tan-y-Mynedd guffawed again, sending a few more of the baby dragons into the air on their tiny wings, coursing and swerving precariously to avoid colliding into one another.

Back on my feet and rubbing my sore backside to gain comfort, I smiled, trying to take it all in good humour. You would think after all these years and the amount of time I spent with this great dragon, I would never get caught out again. I am usually able to avoid this embarrassing mishap but, on this occasion, I questioned my complacency! Perhaps, with other issues on my mind, my guard had dropped. But, whatever the reason, my poor bottom did throb. A baby dragon landed on my shoulder and squawked loudly, its tiny jaws opening and closing with rows of tiny teeth glistening in the natural light created by the seams of quartz crystal which threaded through the rock.

"Well, Crach!" Tan-y-Mynedd launched his head forward. "Methinks you are troubled."

There he goes again, usurping any sense of surprise from my words yet to come if ever allowed to!

"Yes!" Faerydae added. "You do look a little worried!"

"Are you worried, Crach?" Crow chipped in.

"Come, sit down and share your thoughts, dear friend." Fwynedd gesticulated towards a rock I may care to sit upon.

"I think I would prefer to stand," I replied. "My backside is still a little sore." Immediately I realised I should have kept that remark to myself.

"Yes, you should!" agreed Tan-y-Mynedd, guffawing loudly again. Once more, I was the butt end of my own humour. Although I had to smile, what other choice did I have?

"Oh, Crach!" said Crow. "Please tell us what is wrong?"

This was going to be quite a difficult issue to discuss as, in truth, the mutual indiscretions of Crow and Fwynedd were overheard by one of Essex's spies and now resulted in somewhat of a calamity. The King now suspected that not only was it true that dragons still lived in Wales, but there may also be eggs. Every monarch seeks advantages of their enemies and the taming of a dragon to use in war was one such possibility he had no choice but to investigate. He did not know anything in reality, only the whisperings of a clumsy dwarf and an aged shepherd, but it had been enough to compel Henry to dispatch Edmund to search them out. The only possible saving grace in this whole catastrophe which could work to our advantage was the fact that Edmund had been directed to make the investigation. If all is balanced as it should be, the scales of justice would see Lord Edmund fail, yet again. In all honesty, 'by dragon's breath', this was the only possible light in this dark scenario. If Edmund succeeded in his quest, I dread to consider the consequences.

"Ah!" Tan-y-Mynedd raised a scaled eyebrow, a huge golden eye twinkling in the knowledge he now held. But, to my surprise, for a moment or two, the great dragon uttered not a word, although I knew he had once again already read my thoughts, pre-empting any surprise at the point when my thoughts became words—such is the wisdom of the dragon. Why wait for words when one can hear the truth through thought before words are spoken. A tremendous gift to possess over one's enemy but, in my own personal experience, most embarrassing if you are a friend of this dragon.

He broke the silence with a calm dragon voice, as opposed to the brusque tone he often used. "You have something to tell us, Crach?"

"I do," I replied.

The others must have sensed the concern in my voice as Crow, Faerydae, and Fwynedd moved closer, taking their seats on the many moss-covered rocks which covered the cavern floor, whilst the baby dragons played 'baby dragon games'.

They chased each other with a gnash of their small jaws, tiny teeth meeting with tiny tail. They could all fly now and, indeed, all looked to be in fine health. There were seventeen of them and all were growing very quickly. The pile of sheepskins in the corner of the cavern was a testament of their good appetites! An adult dragon can survive for months on end without any food but when they did eat, they did indeed eat! But at this age, they 'ate on demand', as and when their tiny tummies demanded. Given they had Fwynedd the Shepherd as a guardian, there was no shortage of sheep to eat. These seventeen baby dragons were thriving with their personal care overseen by Faerydae, Fwynedd the shepherd providing their sustenance, Tan-y-Mynedd their protector and tutor plus, of course, Crow who was their nursery nurse, giving them hours of fun as they ran circles around him! This was as good a situation as one could hope for and the current threat needed discussion to avoid Edmund discovering their lair or, in fact, any clue to its whereabouts or even any evidence of the dragons' existence.

"I am afraid the English suspect our dragons' nest." I paused as the next piece of information would be very difficult for me to relay.

"How?" Faerydae was the first to remark.

"Words overheard in whispers by a spy of the King's agent, Lord Essex," I replied.

"But how?" asked Fwynedd.

"Yes, how?" chipped in Crow.

Now came the most difficult part. I turned to face Fwynedd and Crow.

"I am afraid, my old friends, from the account I heard, it seems it was stressed by their spy that a dwarf and a shepherd were overheard whispering about dragons in a smoky corner of a hostelry. Furthermore, the descriptions he gave to the King are those of you, old friends. You."

Both Crow and Fwynedd instantly looked very sad and guilty. Fwynedd nervously tugged at his long grey beard.

"Oh—no." he stuttered. "We, here in this cavern, are the only ones who know of them. Apart from the Glyndwr brothers, nobody else is aware."

"Yes, that is true." Crow also looked very sad and guilty but, bless him, Crow always felt guilty about something. His clumsiness might have caused a lot of trouble this time.

The great dragon spoke in truth. "Well, my friends, the fact of the matter at hand means we need to take evasive action. We cannot be unconcerned at all, not by any means. The dragon babies still need a lot of care if they are to survive. We cannot move seventeen baby dragons, it would be impossible, even for me, one who wields dragon magic."

"Yes, what is done cannot be undone, only repaired," said Faerydae.

"How could we have been so foolish as to think our whispering would go unheard?" Fwynedd said with tears in his eyes, as did Crow.

"It is all my fault!" Crow cried. "I was whispering, I promise I was, but I was so excited about all the babies...."

"It is not all your fault," Fwynedd told Crow in kindness and support of his friend. "It was both of us."

"No!" protested Crow. "You were trying to change the subject and get me to shut up. You said we may be whispering but that did not mean someone may not overhear us." The tears now flowed down his cheeks. "And now they have, and you were right, and it is all my fault! Oh, what have I done? And what am I going to do?"

"You, my fine dwarf, will do as you have been doing. You will continue to tend to the babies with the loving care you have always given to them." Tan-y-Mynedd advised Crow. "This is nobody's fault, it is circumstance, and words cannot be undone."

"Come, Crow." I placed my arm around his shoulder and held him close. "You should let this bad feeling go. We must solve our problems."

"Yes, indeed." Tan-y-Mynedd agreed and with a nod from Fwynedd and a smile from Faerydae, we could now discuss what should be done next.

"Do they know where we are, Crach?" Fwynedd questioned.

"They do not," I answered. "The only words given to the King suggested merely the existence of the dragons and this is based on whispers alone."

"Thank goodness for that!" Crow looked a little relieved.

"I think we can all agree that this could have been much worse so perhaps we can breathe a slight sigh of relief. All is not as bad as we at first thought." Fwynedd continued. "As we cannot move seventeen baby dragons and they do not know we are here, I see little point in looking for somewhere else to rear them."

"Indeed, so we can stay here but we need to make sure we cannot be found. Do we know who searches for us, Crach?" Faerydae asked me.

"We do!" I replied. "It is Lord Edmund, an old enemy of mine."

"Ah, him!" Tan-y-Mynedd mused and looked as if he was about to sneeze—but didn't! "The one who is Henry's lapdog! He who thinks we are foolish enough to accept lead where gold should be. This man is a fool!" Tan-y-Mynedd laughed. "A fool!"

This time he did sneeze but we all saw it coming and ducked in time. Even the baby dragons sensed it, so no harm done.

"We are in one of the deepest caverns here and it would be almost impossible to find us unless it was suspected," offered Fwynedd.

Suddenly Crow became agitated.

"The warhorse! He grazes by the entrance to the tunnels." He started to hop from one foot to the other, becoming more agitated by the second.

"We still have time," I said. "Remember, I used the time portal to get here, it will be weeks, if not months before, or if ever, Edmund sniffs anything."

"Apart from his own backside!" chirped up Fwynedd.

"So, move the horse from the entrance and take away the clue, thus it will look simply like yet another cave entrance. Ride her to Sycharth where I will meet you in four days' time," I suggested.

I turned to Crow and held his arm warmly. "Could you do that, Crow?"

"Yes, I could," he nodded enthusiastically. "But, the baby dragons?"

Faerydae held his other arm, giving reassurance and added, "We will protect them, Crow, we will. There is nothing for you to worry about right now."

Crow said his goodbyes and disappeared out of the cavern through the tunnels and up to the surface.

It seemed crucial I should pursue Edmund and I knew just who could find him— Carron the Raven.

Chapter Six

Although it was chilly, the noonday sun hung over the mountains behind the ridge. Shadows danced from the treeline, cascading down the hillside into the valley below. Almost a mirror image on the opposite side of the valley created a beauty only the eye of the beholder may describe with any true feeling and accuracy. It was not too long before I fell asleep and my dreamscape visions unfurled.

Along the drovers' trail at the seat of the valley, a retinue of one hundred English soldiers made their way slowly towards Hawarden. Despatched from a part of Henry's main force, their task to root out the Welsh rebels firmly in mind, they marched on. Twenty or so of the soldiers were mounted cavalry, knights in heavy armour riding huge heavy horses, equally weighed down by breast and flank plates. The face armour of the horses changing their appearance considerably to one of a most evil presence. Some were like gargoyles, others hideous deformities of what would once have been recognisable and beautiful creatures. Riders carried lances and heavy shields, with broadswords secure in belts strapped to waists. Heavy mailed gloves held reins decorated with the insignia of the riders. Whilst they road slowly on, eighty or so foot soldiers clad in chainmail, half of which were archers with long bows stretched across their chests and with quivers full of arrows, followed on. Two wagons drawn by horses brought up the rear of the procession, carrying all the important supplies that armies on the move may need.

The banners of Henry IV flew from their lances and all the soldiers' tabards bore the royal crest. To any onlooker, this looked a force to be reckoned with but Rhodri did not think so. To him, a seasoned warrior, this was an opportunity of the greatest magnitude, a pathway to a quick victory and then, a quick escape.

Owain instructed his men only a few weeks ago to 'Move as ghosts.'

Rhodri had every intention of making this his duty. With only thirty men in his small group, they were vastly outnumbered by over three to one and would seem at a disadvantage when comparing the English army's armour and modern weaponry with their long bows and swords. But what Rhodri and the Welsh army did have, Henry did not, a knowledge of the mountainous landscape which would serve them very well.

"It is a good day for a ride in the Welsh countryside!" Sir Roland remarked to Sir Giles. "A beautiful day and not one Welsh rebel to be seen, I'll be bound!" he laughed.

Sir Giles nodded his head in agreement, causing his visor to fall down, covering his face completely. His reply, now lost inside his armour as the Welshmen attacked.

Well-aimed arrows struck down thirty English soldiers in one swoop and in the first wave of the attack, almost one third perished in an instant. Those not killed outright, lay incapacitated amongst the rocks and bushes. All of the English soldiers ran for what little cover presented itself, whilst the mounted troop simply flayed in every direction, horses rearing, knights being unceremoniously decimated, left lying in heaps on the ground. As the second wave of arrows hit, at least a further twenty English foot soldiers became ghosts, destined to haunt the mountainside for millennia. The remaining English foot soldiers were huddled in a defensive group, benefitting from no cover. Each Welsh arrow found its target with ease, leaving many dead or seriously wounded. Arrow-fire hit soldiers and knights remorselessly for ten minutes as the small Welsh contingent demonstrated their prowess on the battlefield and yet, still unseen.

Sir Giles dismounted, struggled to his feet with the visor now up when down would have been his preference, as an arrow struck him full square in the eye. Sir Giles fell back to the ground for the last time.

Sir Roland still sat on his horse until another reared and collided with him, bringing both riders to the ground. Sir Roland struggled to his feet and looked around at what was now left of his command. Most of the foot soldiers and bowmen were dead or mortally wounded. The dozen or so that were not, made haste to the hills with the wind at their backs. At least ten knights, now on foot, survived but were still unable to see their enemy. Another hail of arrows and three more knights died where they stood.

"Now!" Rhodri yelled with all the voice he could muster.

Thirty proud and strong Welshmen, led by Rhodri, descended on the remaining English, with half coming down one side of the valley and likewise opposite. Sir Roland quickly realised they had been caught in a very effective trap and the speed of the arrow volley gave the impression of their attackers numbering a hundred men or more.

Surprise being the last of Sir Roland's emotions as Rhodri confronted him, broadsword in hand. He slashed at Sir Roland, narrowly missing his shoulder, bringing the blade back at speed, Sir Roland parried with effect but felt the strength of his opponent wielding the blade. In his mind, he knew here was a strong warrior and this was a fight for his life. Again, Rhodri slashed, following his blow by kicking Sir Roland in the groin. Protected by his armour, Sir Roland lurched back, regained his stance just in time, and parried another strong blow from his opponent's broadsword. Quickly he glanced around, never had he seen so many decimated by so few in such a short space of time. His comrades were fighting three or four opponents each. He thought to himself, it is only a matter of time. He did not see the blade as it struck him in the side, entering a gap where his armour was unsecure. He felt it go deep, piercing his lung and heart. Sir Roland gasped as his eyes rolled and he crumpled lifelessly to the ground.

Rhodri looked at the carnage that was once the proud English soldiery. All lay dead or wounded.

"Shall we kill the wounded, Rhodri?" Goch, a black-smith from Llangollen, asked.

"No!" He looked sternly at the dead and then at the others moaning and whimpering in their death-throws. "If they survive, their tales will fill any that may march upon us again with fear. If they die, so be it. If the pigs eat them, so be it."

Turning around for one last time, Rhodri simply raised his arm and ordered: "We go!" The thirty Welsh rebels ran back up the hillside and disappeared back into the forest from whence they came.

My dreamscape shuddered.

***

Lord Essex sat, perplexed, listening to a wandering deserter from the battle, now returned, as he told his version of the slaughter.

"My Lord, there were hundreds and we were outnumbered three to one! Within a quarter of one hour, our troop was no more. Sir Giles was brought down too! Dead, my Lord—dead."

Essex realised that this would be difficult news to give to the King as the inner workings of his regal mind were twisted and warped by an illusion of nothing more than power. The more power he held, the more he wanted and sought. He considered that to rule Wales was a question not to be asked, this is what he would do and therefore is all anyone need consider.

There was a strong ring of castles around Snowdonia and most served Henry so he thought it should be relatively easy to quell the rebellion, after all, he did have ten thousand soldiers on both foot and horse. His plan was to hunt down the rebels, catch Glyndwr and then reinforce the castles with his most seasoned soldiers.

***

The King, ensconced in his chair with a full goblet in hand, toyed a piece of meat with the point of a dagger, rolling it around his plate. Lords Leicester and Waverly sat at the table with the King and their spirits seemed high. Henry appeared thoughtful and raising the goblet to his lips, took a full long gulp. Remnants of the wine dribbled down his chin, dripping onto his tunic, adding to previous stains.

The tent flap opened and a Sergeant at Arms stepped in, bowed and announced: "Lord Essex requests an audience with the King.""Yes, yes.... Tell him to come in." Henry gave a cursory wave with the dagger, confirming his command. When the Sergeant at Arms saluted and withdrew, Essex entered with a bustle, looking anxious and extremely perturbed. It was late in the evening in very cold October, yet beads of sweat dripped from his beard, his normal composure had disappeared and was replaced with trembling anxiety. Henry, Leicester, and Waverly all seemed surprised to see Essex in such a state of mind. If there was one thing to be relied upon, Essex was always the statesman, but not tonight.

"What is it, Essex? You are in a bad way, man, and we are disturbed by your demeanour. Tell me, hold back not from your King, I would demand an answer immediately!" Henry stabbed the dagger into the table with a thud and left it shaking in situ as he banged his fist down to reinforce the royal command.

"My King, I come with grave news from near Hawarden." Essex lowered his gaze.

"Hawarden?" Leicester queried. "Is that not where Sir Roland and Sir Giles rode with a hundred strong?"

Waverly leaned forward and confirmed to Leicester. "Yes, it is, Leicester, twenty knights, and horses, eighty archers and foot soldiers with pike and sword."

"A formidable force, I think we can agree," added Henry with a gratuitous smile.

Essex started to tremble when the King said the word 'formidable'."And so, Essex?" Henry tapped his fingers expectantly on the goblet in his hand.

"All dead, My King—all dead."

Leicester stood in surprise. "What?" he exclaimed.

"You heard!" Henry barked turning on Leicester with venom. "All dead!"

A goblet flew through the air as his temper rose, narrowly missing Essex's head.

"Are there no survivors?" asked Waverly.

"A dozen, no more. Stragglers and deserters who ran when the Welsh struck," replied Essex.

"How can we believe the words of cowards?" Henry, livid now, was red in the face and the veins in his neck pulsated. His anger knew no bounds in situations such as this. "Have you hung them, Essex?"

"No, My Lord, not yet. I have listened to all their stories and all seem to agree they were vastly outnumbered by three to one. They did not see any of the rebels until they charged down the hillside, appearing from nowhere. Before that, wave after wave of arrows took the men down. No cover, you see, My Lord. They were ambushed and slaughtered. The rebels disappeared with not a sign of them ever having being there at all, except for our dead and mortally wounded."

"Hang them!" ordered Henry.

CHAPTER SEVEN

Owain was sitting by the fire looking quite bemused, and who could blame him after sitting for the best part of three hours whilst I brought him up to date with recent events? So far, all the planning had worked out just as envisaged, everything, as surely as day is day and night is night. Tudur had ridden to Anglesey whilst Owain's other captains had led their various bands and successfully raided and captured Oswestry and Welshpool. Within a few short weeks since September 14th, our small army had captured seven of the major towns, striking fear into the English lords. Rhodri had swooped and ambushed a troop of one hundred of Henry's finest soldiers and killed most of them.

"You did tell them to strike hard, fast and to be as ghosts," I stated. "Our men were good to the artistry of your word."

Smiling, I asked Owain to pass me the water jug. All this talking had made me as dry as a pine forest in the heart of summer. "And, My Lord, thus far 'The Prophecy' is correct, not a man have we lost. Not one!"

Owain passed me the water jug, together with an apple. "Quench your thirst, Crach. It is a good story for our children's children to tell at the time between times in years to come."

"It is, My Lord, and, of course, so far the crisis with the dragons has subsided somewhat."

"Well, with that wimp, Edmund, in pursuit, I do not think we need worry too much."

He passed me the wine but I declined, silently shaking my head.

"So, we are plagued by him yet again!" I said after drinking a long draught of water. It cooled my throat, gliding well-needed lubricant to an over-worked voice. "Although I think we do have more serious problems ahead with the dragons," I remarked. "Problems much more challenging than those of Sir Edmund. There are seventeen baby dragons, Owain, and they are growing very quickly. Whilst it will be two or three years before they are fully grown like Tan-y-Mynedd, they are getting bigger by the day."

"I see," said Owain. "I hadn't thought of that. Seventeen flying, fire-breathing dragons. Some fire power, eh, Crach?"

Question or statement? I was unsure, but certainly, a fact that could not be denied. If the dragons decided to go into battle supporting Owain, the army would be invincible. So far, Tan-y-Mynedd avoided discussing such involvement as the 'Ways of Men' gave dragons great displeasure and in the grand dragon's opinion, best to be avoided. However, Tan-y-Mynedd also served 'The Prophecy' and as a member of the Council of Blue Stone such a decision as to whether the dragons should go to war may not be only his. Still, this was some time in the future. The baby dragons had some growing to do yet and Tan-y-Mynedd much to instruct them in dragon law. But inevitably the question would be asked.

Owain leaned back in the chair and toasted his feet in front of the fire. "What, in heaven's name, will happen next, dear Crach? Everything moves with the speed of breath."

"As it should, my Prince," I replied. "As it should."

"You say Carron the Raven is searching for Edmund?" Owain asked as he curled his toes in the warmth.

"I did, My Lord. He knows brother and sister ravens both in the King's castle and elsewhere. Edmund will be found." I sneezed and hoped this was not the beginning of an early autumn cold. "And soon, I am sure."

"And when he is found, Crach?"

"A good question," I replied.

CHAPTER EIGHT

Carron the Raven cawed and fluttering huge black wings, landed on my shoulder and as usual, dug sharp claws into my flesh! He nibbled at my ear-ring as is his custom, before sticking a sharp beak into my ear and whispering. "We have found your Lord Edmund. A brother raven spied him on the Welsh border. He travels with two others, large brutish types. All three are disguised as merchants. They ride at speed and are asking questions and offering rewards for any information about 'dragon eggs." He withdrew his beak from my ear and fluttered feathers. The beak returned. "It seems he is trying to get people to speak with him and to believe he is a merchant and collector of curios. He tells them he has heard stories of 'dragon eggs' and searches in Wales because it is the 'Land of the Dragon'."

Carron jumped from my shoulder, flew a short distance, alighting on a branch in a nearby tree and pecked around randomly in an aimless fashion.

Well, it seems Lord Edmund is as subtle as ever in his approach to the quest given to him by the King of England. Considering nobody knew anything, he was on a pointless task. No matter how much reward was offered, no matter how many questions he asked, there would be no true answers as there were none to give.

English merchants would be easy to track. I heaved a sigh of relief and thanked the universe for Edmund's ineptitude. The dragon babies were safe, at least for now.

Merlina, my trusty old mare, was tethered to the tree where Carron had landed on the branch above her head. She nervously twitched and flicked her tail. Carron flew down, landing on her back. The mare stamped her hoof several times, nodding her head in frustration rather than compliance. Horse and raven had known each other, or should I say tolerated each other, for many years. Untying her reins, I rolled down my little ladder and climbed up, joining Carron on her faithful back. I had to meet Crow later that day, along with the warhorse he was riding to Sycharth. Pulling the collar tight around my neck to keep out the biting wind, I gently pressed my heels into Merlina's flanks and off we trotted, her tail swishing with delight as Carron took to the air and flew alongside us. Goodness, it was turning very cold and it would not be too long before the snows came yet again.

For a brief moment, I considered Henry and his army in all their finery, with heavy horses who were so unfamiliar with our land. They would not fare well in the deep winter with little knowledge of our terrain and probably being ill-equipped to deal with the fierce weather conditions in the mountains but, of course, this would be to our advantage. It seemed to me the winter season was as much a warrior for Wales as we were. Only the summer may give some respite and they seemed to be travelling over well-established routes, easy to watch and hear about. Our land was criss-crossed with drovers' trails which we knew well, Henry's men would never see us coming when it was time for our attack.

The wind picked up as I rode on, drops of rain fell and Carron flew high into the sky. He soared from view, but he would be back.

Riding through the gates at Sycharth, Emrys, the 'Keeper of the Gate', raised his hand in welcome.

"Ho, Master Crach!" he smiled. "Looks as if the heavens may open and we will be in for a good drenching."

"It looks to be so, Emrys," I responded, looking up at the dark grey sky, serving to confirm his words. I nodded and rode on towards the house.

Riding into the courtyard, a welcome sight met my eyes. There, tethered at the stable wall, stood the magnificent black warhorse. She had her nose deep in a bag of oats, long mane quivering with satisfaction as her tail swished from left to right. In front of the stable, sat on a mound of straw with knees tucked under a familiar chin, snored Crow. As good as his word, my old friend had succeeded in making the journey from Ffestiniog. Mind you, he had a fine mount upon which to make the journey. I guided Merlina towards the stable when suddenly, out of the sky from absolutely nowhere, came Carron, landing on the top of my head. Fortunately, the hood prevented his talons from scratching my scalp, or worse! He fluttered down onto the saddle in front of me and squawked loudly, making Merlina stumble and Crow wake with a start, falling off the straw with a clump. Staggering to his feet, the old dwarf caught a glimpse of me and immediately woke from a post-slumbering trance!

"Crach!" Crow ran towards me. Taking Merlina's reins, he looked up at me and said, "Well, we both made it here then, just as we agreed?"

"Did you encounter any problems on your journey from Ffestiniog?" I asked him.

"None at all," he answered. "Remarkably, I had not even one mishap. I usually do, as you know."

"Well, not until you fell off the straw mound!" I remarked, smiling.

"Oh, yes. I was asleep." Crow responded, looking sheepish.

"I know, Crow," I said kindly. "When did you arrive?" I asked as I rolled down the ladder and dismounted from Merlina's back.

"At midday," Crow replied. "I made very good time on this fine mare. She is, indeed, a joy to ride. Her stride is so perfect, I almost fell asleep in the saddle!"

"I am glad you didn't!" I replied.

Crow led Merlina towards the stable, relieved her of the saddle and tethered her next to the warhorse. Merlina looked so small against the large mare, the top of her head not even reaching the warhorse's neck. Crow poured oats into a nosebag and hooked it over Merlina's head. She wasted no time in filling her empty tummy. There they stood, both horse and pony, resting, relaxed and eating, which was just what they both deserved.

I hooked my arm over Crow's shoulder and we walked slowly towards the great house. It was important Owain learned Edmund was in Wales again, searching for the eggs in the most ludicrous of ways. Edmund held specific commands to search quietly and avoid raising suspicions. Well, he already achieved the opposite so our previous discussions and opinions proved correct.

Walking up the steps to the main door, it suddenly burst open and there appeared Tudur, clad in partial armour. He looked happy and content, with a huge smile spread across his rather stained face. Remnants of mud from hard riding and dried blood from hard fighting stained his face like a battlefield. His hair hung greasy and matted, coated with dried blood.

"Crach! Good to see you! And is this Crow, the clumsy dwarf, I see before me?"

"It is," replied Crow, bowing as low as his now aged back would allow.

"Rise up, Dwarf. You have no need to bow here!" Tudur told him as he leaned down and took Crow by the shoulders, helping him to stand straight again.

"Thank you, my Lord." Crow looked embarrassed.

"You look a little battle-worn, Tudur!" I remarked.

"We are returned from Welshpool and Oswestry, Crach. It was a bloody fight but we took both towns well. One or two have been wounded, but not one Welshman is dead!" he informed me with delight.

"A good result!" I responded, while in my mind I knew it was only a matter of time before a Welshman would be killed.

"You are looking for my brother, friends?" he enquired.

"We are, Tudur," I answered.

"He is in The Great Hall with Iolo Gogh who is here with news from the Bishop of St. Asaph."

"Ah, I wonder what this news is. We have news of our own to share as well," I said.

"Well, I will see you at dinner tonight, will I?" Tudur

asked as he leapt down the last two steps. "I go to clean away the battle and bathe, Crach. I go!" With that, Tudur stepped out towards the bathhouse, whistling to himself.

'Oh, such joy there is in victory,' I thought *'But sadness awaits in defeat and victory comes at a price.'*

"Let's go, Crow."

We stepped through the doorway into The Great Hall.

Iolo was very old now but he continued to travel the country with news of the day, scripted into poems and rhyme. He had been the younger brother of my old teacher, Myrddin Goch ap Cwnwrig, first known to me under his English name of Master Healan, who now served the Council of Blue Stone through the spirit kingdom as, indeed, did Llwyd ap Crachan Llwyd, to whom I had been an apprentice before my journey with 'The Prophecy' began.

Entering The Great Hall always made me feel even smaller than I am! Its grandeur and splendour adorned the walls and huge oak beams criss-crossed the ceiling. The leaded windows gave much light and the sun shared the room for most of the day—that is if the sun did shine! Banners of Wales and the ancient princes draped across a large oak fireplace which had a grate so large, it was almost like another room—well, at least it would be to a person of similar stature to me! A large oak table still stood at one end of The Great Hall where it had been left after the trial of Edmund and Usk. It was as if the trial had been held just a few months ago. Gone now were the cages that held them though.

Owain sat by the fire, toasting his feet, boots cast aside in the name of comfort. Old man Gogh sat opposite him. He really was very old now and his stooped shoulders seemed to be having trouble holding his head upon them. He was also very thin and his gown hung on him as it may a skeleton.

Although aged, the face of Iolo Gogh came very much alive when the brightness and light in his eyes met with mine. Such life and light still shone in this old man and also wisdom that I am sure will last on for centuries through his words, recorded in his own hand for all to read, for all time.

He raised his head as we walked into the hall. "Is this two dwarfs I see in one place or are these old eyes troubled with double vision?"

Owain turned and saw us. "Crach and Crow! Come in and warm yourselves by this great fire."

It was, indeed, a great fire. A pyramid of large logs blazed with spluttering sparks rising up the chimney.

"Did you see Tudur, Crach?" Owain questioned.

"I did, my Lord. As we came in," I answered. "I may say he looked as if he has been in the thick of the fighting."

"Indeed, he has," Owain said. "You know my brother when there is a fight to be had, he is there in the midst of it with his sword sharpened!"

Iolo Gogh struggled to his feet and it was immediately plain to see just how crooked his back had become. Leaning on a cane, he slowly walked towards me.

"Well I never, Crach Ffinnant." The old man smiled and his face lit up.

"Master Gogh," I returned and gave him a courteous bow. "It has been some time since we last met. I do hope the planets keep you well."

"Well, they do not protect us from the years as they pass by and the toll they bring upon our physical being, that is certain, yet my mind is as sharp as it ever was. Old age is our worst enemy, Crach, and one you may confront someday." The old man looked at Crow with a knowing expression. "And you, Master Dwarf? Let me remember—you—now let me think. Your name is that of a bird—a blackbird.... Yes, I have it! Crow. It is Crow, I believe?"

"It is, Master Gogh," confirmed Crow who, for some strange reason, started shuffling from one foot to the other.

"As you say, bard," Owain interjected. "Nothing wrong with your memory."

Iolo Gogh remained standing and turning to Owain, said, "Well, I must take leave, my Lord. I have enjoyed my visit to you, as always." The old man scratched his chin. "I will record my visit in verse, as is my custom," he added.

"We shall look forward to it, old bard. Will we not, Crach?" Owain said, including me in his farewell to the old man.

"We shall, my Lord. It has been grand to see you again." I said, taking Iolo by the arm and gripping him fondly.

"It has, young Crach. Although, even you are not so young anymore!" He smiled and we all laughed. Even Crow, who had calmed a little, giggled under his breath.

"I fear your visit has been all too short," Owain said, "but I thank you sincerely for bringing the information from The Bishop of St Asaph. It is good to know all is in hand."

"It is, my Lord," Iolo replied. "It is!"

As the old man shuffled from the room with his back bent, I wondered if I would ever see him again. He was becoming extremely frail.

"And so, Crach!" Owain clapped his hands together, leaned forward towards the fire and warmed them by the flames. "What news?"

"We have heard of Edmund, my Lord," I answered. "Carron brought us news from the borders where it seems, he is much less discreet about his quest than his King may like."

"Ah! Shooting his fat mouth off like aimless arrows from

an empty quiver again, is he?" Owain continued to warm his hands.

"He is!" I smiled. "He feigns the guise of a merchant who is seeking dragon eggs and is offering rewards for information."

"Is he alone, Crach?" chipped in Crow.

"No, Crow. He travels with two brutish riders and they are just a little too well armed to truly pass themselves off as merchants and they, like Edmund, have strong English accents and ride splendid horses from the royal stable."

Owain laughed loudly and called for wine.

"We should celebrate the fact that he continues to be a complete buffoon," Owain said.

Chapter Nine

Edmund dismounted from a black stallion and tethered it outside the hostelry. They arrived just in time as the heavens opened and a torrential downpour flooded the ground within minutes.

"You, boy!" Edmund shouted at the stable lad. "Bed our steeds down and feed them well. And don't forget to give them a good brush down or I will want to know the reason why not!" He threw a farthing in the boy's direction before disappearing through the large door into the hostelry.

The establishment was more of a coach house than a hostelry and was in the village of Hawarden. It was run by an Englishman who was loyal to the King.

"Good evening, Sirs," he greeted the three strangers. "Will you be wanting a room for the night?"

"We will need two rooms, Landlord." Edmund asserted. "I want your finest for myself and another for these two to share." He casually gesticulated to his companions who stood behind him.

"You are merchants, Sir?" the Landlord enquired.

"You are an observant fellow," Edmund smiled. "We are, indeed, and are on a quest of great importance, my man!"

"Well, Sir, I will show you to your rooms and then perhaps I may serve you with some hot food, together with some ale."

"Wine for me," hailed Edmund. "Ale will suffice for them."

Sam Hetherington had been the Landlord of this coach house for years and witnessed many changes. The worst, of course, being the rebellion which threatened to disturb the peace across the whole country. He was not a fool and had seen it coming. Although loyal to the King, he was loyal to himself in the first instance and enjoyed friendships with a number of Welshmen. Sam liked to see both sides of an argument, choosing the side that suited himself. His loyalty was primarily to Sam Hetherington.

In the winter of his fiftieth year, he could not abide trouble and had a good nose for avoiding it. He was assisted in being able to ignore any problems by drinking a good deal of his own ale. His head was balding but he sprouted grey hair, like clouds floating over his ears. Sam's nose was almost purple and his complexion seemed a little more than merely rosy. He may have been portly but he was still very strong, as one may expect from a man who humps barrels of ale around all day, every day.

As Edmund and his companions returned down the stairs, Sam was rubbing greasy hands on the apron strapped tightly around his large paunch.

"A table beside the fire, Sir?" Sam waved his arm, gesturing his offer.

"Yes, indeed!" Edmund was almost shouting. "Wine for me, ale for them!" he instructed while clapping his hands together and moving towards the warmth of the fire.

His two companions were almost like shadows, saying nothing, apart from the odd grunt. Choosing to leave Edmund to his high and mighty self, they sat in a corner, near to the fire but away from their Master's arrogance.

Sam brought the ale and wine over, being careful to serve Edmund first. He thought he may have the measure of this guest and was not going to tempt providence by upsetting him in any way. After all, he was a rich merchant and certainly had the look of one, so his money was as good as anyone else's.

"We have good lamb pottage, also bread and cheese, my Lord, if that would suit?" Sam waited for Edmund to reply.

"Good. Yes, and plenty of it, if you please. I have not eaten since breakfast."

His two companions heard his words, but he did not hear theirs as one said to the other, "He ate enough at breakfast for three men, greedy sod."

"He is an arrogant prick," the other remarked.

Sam Hetherington served his guests with food, hot and plentiful, before busying himself wiping the top of his counter. This was not a busy night for Sam with only one other guest staying overnight besides Edmund and his companions, although there were several locals who sat drinking ale, muttering quietly over their tankards.

Edmund pushed the plate away with not a morsel left and drained his goblet. "More wine, if you please, Landlord!" he shouted.

"Coming right away, Sir." Sam picked up a flagon from

the bar and hobbled over to Edmund's table. "Would you like me to pour for you, Sir?" Sam enquired.

"No. Leave the flagon with me and serve them more ale," Edmund ordered, giving a cursory backward glance at his 'shadows' in the corner. "Now, I would have questions of you, my good man, but I wonder if you will have any answers for me?"

"I would not know till you ask your questions," Sam said sarcastically.

"I am not sure I like your tone, churl!" Edmund was back in his favourite persona, as a bully.

One of his 'shadows' stood and looked menacingly at Sam Hetherington. Sam realised he should have kept his comments to himself so in his most servile manner, began an attempt at grovelling his way out of this uncomfortable situation.

The 'shadow' sat down and Edmund took another long swig, draining his goblet.

"There, we will say no more," Edmund arrogantly said. "Now, my questions, if you please?"

"Yes, Sir," Sam almost whispered, wishing to avoid any further wrath from this surly merchant if, indeed, he was a merchant at all.

"Dragons. I seek dragons. What can you tell me?"

Sam tried to subdue the burst of laughter stuck at the back of his throat. "Dragons, Sir?"

"Yes, dragons! You are not deaf, of that I am sure. Why do you repeat my words?" Edmund blustered.

"They say there used to be dragons about here but that was over one hundred years ago, Sir. No such thing anymore though." Sam wiped his sweaty hands down the front of his apron. "I, myself, do not believe there were ever such creatures," he added.

"Oh, don't you now!" Edmund was getting riled again. "It seems to me you think you know more than your betters!"

"Not at all, Sir. Please do forgive me." Sam backed away and bowed in respect, hoping he could defuse his guest's temper.

"You, folk!" Edmund shouted as he stood, addressing everybody in the room. "What do you know of dragons hereabouts?"

Without exception, everybody became quite hysterical, laughing and spitting ale everywhere.

"He is balmy!" came one voice.

"Deranged," said another.

"Creatures of mystic tales," added someone else.

"No such bloody thing!" the remarks continued.

Edmund never liked being laughed at but when he caught sight of his companions also laughing at him, it was just too much. Clearly feeling outnumbered on every front, he withdrew in temper and stormed upstairs to bed.

One of the companions whispered in a low voice. "Told you, this is all a waste of time," he laughed. "Dragons!"

CHAPTER TEN

News of the attacks on the English spread across Wales as would a wildfire in summer. Of course, as with all news, by the time the stories had been heard and retold by many, embellishment by subsequent tellers of the tale made it sound as if the English had been totally defeated, which was by no means true. The rebellion had only just begun and with Christmas behind us, this was no time for complacency. King Henry had an army of ten thousand men who had marched into Wales. The snows were hard this year and came early. We were used to hard weather, but the English were not so accustomed to it. We had been commanded by Owain we must use this to our advantage. Plans were afoot to do just that and I knew I had much still to prepare for.

The baby dragons were now six months old and about the

size of a Wolfhound, although with wings and much sharper teeth than a hound! As you can imagine, work was now very challenging in the nursery. Faerydae, Fwynedd, and Crow worked night and day but the larger the babies became, the more difficult they were to care for.

My first task was to discuss with Tan-y-Mynedd how their teachings were progressing. It was a source of great anxiety to me whenever I thought about the seventeen dragons in waiting. Tan-y-Mynedd certainly had his work cut out, but then, perhaps, his lack of patience may, or may not, be a strength in this situation. Only time would tell.

Lord Edmund was still blundering from village to village and there were now stories of a mad English merchant who babbled about dragons. He was rapidly becoming a source of great amusement to many and an embarrassment to a few. I am sure the King must have heard of his exploits by now. I pondered what he may think and then considered that surely Edmund's head would not be on his shoulders for very much longer, but then he did seem to have an abundance of luck. Still, the fact of the matter remains, whilst ever he continued in this way, the favours were all in our court. If only he knew the truth, I think he may truly go mad, never to return to sanity!

Owain's army had achieved much in such a short time but now, as the spring of 1401 approached, he had his eyes on greater things. Wales contained many English strongholds, many castles where their lords dispersed judgement upon the Welsh and collected English taxes. It was time to take the castles. I knew when I cast my runes that this year would be pivotal in uniting the Welsh in our struggle against the tyranny of King Henry. My readings told me of success in battle, at least for now. The thing that worried me the most was my 'cast for the future' as the unrest seemed to go on and on with no end in sight. Some things a seer must keep to himself, and this was one of them.

I heard disturbing news from Carron the Raven who informed me Erasmus, the old court wizard, had been found in Glastonbury and, at Henry's command, was being escorted to North Wales. He was now quite ancient in years and had served a number of Kings. I prayed that Henry would treat him kindly.

Now it was time to make a decision I had been putting off, and that was to finally let Merlina retire to the paddock at Sycharth. I now rode the warhorse who I had named Cwtch. She was a very solid mare and when riding her, I felt two major things. One, I was a long way from the ground and two, it was a long way to fall! Thankfully, she was getting used to the time portals and there had been no further mishap, as on the first occasion. I often wondered what those English soldiers who had no knowledge of time portals must have thought as she disappeared in front of their eyes.

So, it was now time to visit Tan-y-Mynedd.

Chapter Eleven

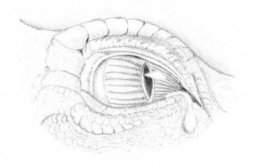

"This is a time of great strain on an old dragon, Crach! Of that, there is no doubt!" Tan-y-Mynedd shook his head in resignation. "Like all adolescents, some behave, some do not. I must say, I am feeling sorry for dear Crow in his task of caring for them. All the young dragons love him as they would their real mother. It is both funny and interesting to watch as he tries to keep them in order."

"And how goes their teaching?" I asked Tan-y-Mynedd.

"Much the same," the great dragon replied, with a twinkle in his eye. "Some are quick to learn, others are slower. And some, well, two, in particular, are not interested at all. They keep wandering off down into the deeper caverns instead of learning how to use their dragon skills. Still, it could be worse."

I am sure I saw him smile.

"They are flying very well, although only in the cathedral cavern at the moment as it is the largest," he sighed. "I will have to take them out at night before long but I can't take them all at once, so my task is great, Crach."

"You are certainly kept very busy, old friend. I do not envy you the work you have in hand."

I did not need to say much else as he knew that I understood. Don't forget, dragons know what one is thinking, especially a dragon with the maturity and experience of Tan-y-Mynedd.

"To be honest," Tan-y-Mynedd added. "In another six months they will come into their own, so not too much longer to go in the scheme of things."

"And then?" I queried.

"We will see." He said "But I worry for the future as I do not feel we should interfere in the ways of men. They are cruel and unjust. Although, I will admit that Owain Glyndwr is a rare exception to this rule."

"Of course," I interjected. "'The Prophecy' is as pure in intent as it is in content".

"But you do realise, Crach," he paused. "If the Council of Blue Stone do so order us to join the rebellion, it may alter the future irrevocably. It is better we shy away in the underworld from the eyes of men. Consider, if you will, there will be nineteen dragons in all—myself and Dan-y-Ogof, if he is found alive, plus the youngsters. We will be a formidable force to be reckoned with, of that there is no doubt. We could lay flat all the English cities, slaughter all the English people. But then what?" A tear appeared in the corner of the great dragon's golden eye. "We would inevitably become sport again for the huntsmen. And I know what you are going to say, Crach. You are about to say that Glyndwr would never allow it but, sadly, I say to you, he could not prevent it. What penalties may be ordered for slaying a dragon? Whatever they may be, there is nothing in the universe to give credence to such a thing. No, I am certain we must banish ourselves to the deeper caverns. It is for the best, of that I am sure. In fact, there is no doubt." The tear dropped to the cave floor with a splash.

Faerydae had been listening quietly and she gently touched my arm to attract attention. "He is right you know, Crach. Tan-y-Mynedd is right."

"I know. I have feared these times since the eggs first hatched." I said. "But 'The Prophecy' states categorically the 'Rise of the Dragon' is twofold in meaning—both our country and the species. Owain has the ancient bloodline of the Dragon Princes of Wales—eight hundred years of royal princes." I paused. "But I do not disagree. Perhaps I need to try and work a way through this."

"No!" boomed Tan-y-Mynedd. "'*We*' will work our way through this. You are not responsible for any of this, Crach. You are, as I am also, merely a pawn in the path of 'The Prophecy' to which we serve."

"As well we might be," Fwynedd the Shepherd spoke from the shadows. "But I agree with you all. Surely our role is, as it has been up until now, to take care of the dragons. I know my loyalty lies here and there is no need to question Crow as to where his loyalty lies, as we all know where that is."

"Yes," I said. "We may all agree with each other but if the Council of Blue Stone decides differently, then we have a crisis on the horizon."

"And we will meet the problem if and when it arises," interjected the great dragon. "We have enough to do right now. Remember the rogue Edmund roams the countryside, seeking news of our existence and also remember that we must maintain secrecy at all costs."

Just as he paused for breath, a baby dragon awoke, fluttered its wings, raised a scaled head, opened its now much bigger jaws and squawked. My, how they were growing, day by day. Within just a few minutes, all seventeen baby dragons were awake and hungry. Fwynedd brought six sheep from the stable into an outer chamber which had been set aside especially for the purpose of feeding the youngsters. They were ravenous creatures and soon there was only the fleece left of the sheep. After feasting, they found their own space, laid down with folded wings and went back to sleep.

"Well, all is quiet for now," I smiled.

CHAPTER TWELVE

I sat with Owain and Tudur in front of the fire in The Great Hall. It roared in flame as the seasoned oak burned well, giving off tremendous heat. We certainly needed it as there was snow waist-high outside and everything had come to a halt for the present.

"This is the sort of weather when time portals are more than useful. Eh, Crach?" Tudur laughed.

"Whilst they are useful in any weather, you still have to get to them, such as trudging through the snow," I remarked. "So, there are still some disadvantages."

We all smiled.

We dined very well and this dwarf had certainly eaten an ample sufficiency. I had eaten so much, I could hardly move. Tudur, as usual, was a little worse the wear for wine and was making jokes about everything said by us.

"Would you like some wine, Crach?" Owain offered me the jug but I declined. Wine always made me feel sleepy and I needed to keep my wits about me. Eating so much had already slowed me down. I had been somewhat indulgent this evening.

"Come on, Crach, you are not going anywhere. It's snowing outside. Have some wine and warm your insides." Tudur offered me a goblet which I again declined.

"Leave him alone, Tudur. It will be all the more for you!" Owain playfully kicked at Tudur's leg.

"Indeed, that is true, Brother. I will take your wise counsel."

With that comment, Tudur leaned over and took the jug from the table, filling his goblet to the brim. Putting it to his lips, Tudur took a deep gulp, followed by another. Tilting it skywards, tipping his head back, Tudur proceeded to drain the wine, immediately refilling the large goblet.

"Well, it has been a long day, my Lords." I stood up. "I must away to my sheepskins, my dreams call me."

"The fire is alight in your room, Crach." Owain stood and patted me warmly on my shoulder. "You have dined well and now you must rest. Neither of us is as young as we were. In fact, I often wonder where all the years have gone and what those in front of us may yet hold."

"Thank you." I gripped his arm tenderly and bade them both goodnight.

"Sleep well, my fine Dwarf," Tudur called after me.

"Have more respect, Brother!" Owain chastised him.

"It was only a joke! Drink up."

I heard his goblet hit the table as I left the hall.

My room was toasty warm with the fire blazing and my

cot was snugly covered in sheepskins. I threw some water onto my face from the bowl on the dresser, removed my boots, throwing them onto the floor along with my jerkin, and climbed into a cosy cot. Leaning back, I stretched over and snuffed out the candle before sinking my head into the pillow. I stared at the ceiling in the half-light, watching shadows dance here and there. Taking a deep breath, I sighed and with my eyelids heavy, sleep overtook me immediately.

A loud knock on the oak door and a squeak of its hinges roused me from my deep slumber. A voice calling me as the door creaked again woke me completely. It was Emrys.

"Master Crach! Our Prince requests your presence in The Great Hall immediately. It is a matter of great importance, I am to say. A messenger has arrived with urgent news, I am to tell you."

"Yes, yes, Emrys!" I said, wiping the sleep from my eyes. "Have I overslept?"

"No, Sir. It is not yet light. Dawn is some time away yet," Emrys answered me as I was attempting to pull on my boots.

"Let me help," Emrys offered his assistance.

"Thank you," I said, becoming fully awake.

Lifting my legs, one at a time, Emrys effortlessly slipped on my boots. "There we are, Sir. Boots on."

"Thank you, Emrys. I am grateful to you. Let me drink some water and then off we will go."

I drank from the water jug and feeling refreshed, said to Emrys, "It is an odd time to bring a message. It is the middle of the night, in the middle of winter!"

"Must be very important, Master Crach," he said.

"Indeed, it must," I replied as he opened the door for me to go down the stairs to The Great Hall.

Apart from torches giving light to secluded corners of the

stairway, all was in darkness. Ahead of us, light seeped from beneath the door and when Emrys opened it, I was greeted by the sight of a bedraggled messenger, sitting by the huge fire. He drank hot mead whilst warming his chilled bones.

"Ah, Crach." Owain stood as we entered. "The day starts before it has begun!"

I nodded in silence, taking in the early hour.

"The messenger brings important news," Owain informed me as he warmed his rear by the fire. "Henry has turned his army around. He finds the winter too harsh but he has appointed Harry Hotspur to take control of our country."

Upon hearing the name 'Hotspur', I immediately became fully alert. "Hotspur!" I repeated.

"Yes, Crach, Hotspur," Owain confirmed.

Harry Hotspur was a seasoned warrior, having served in many campaigns over the years. He knew of the problems in Wales and also of the difficulties Henry had created. How could he not? His reputation travelled ahead of him. His real name was Henry Percy and he was knighted by King Edward III in 1377. We had fought alongside him in Scotland under the banners of Richard II. That was sixteen years ago and since then, he had added many more conquests to his reputation. He had been well rewarded by Henry IV for turning against Richard II. It was eighteen months ago that Henry Bolingbroke became King of England and appointed Hotspur as High Sheriff of Flintshire. Now he had been promoted again.

"He has been given the post of Royal Lieutenant to North Wales," Owain said.

"Aw! 'Hell in a Thunderstorm'!" Tudur exclaimed, wiping dreams away from his tired and somewhat bloodshot eyes. "He cannot be trusted—he betrayed Richard."

"Yes, he did," affirmed Owain.

"This is a man who has been wounded, captured, ransomed and risen to dizzy heights. It is by his own tenacity that he still survives. I do not like him but am aware he is a formidable adversary," interjected Owain.

"You know, my friends," I began as I moved closer towards the fire to warm my chilled feet and hands. "I see him turning on the King as he turned on Richard. He is in his prime at not yet fifty years of age. Believe me, he has his eyes set firmly on the Crown."

"You may be right, Crach," Owain said, pouring a small ale. Tudur gulped at a goblet of wine left over from last evening. "With Hotspur doing the King's bidding, we must be careful. He is a shrewd man."

There seemed little point in returning to bed this night with dawn but an hour away, so I took an early breakfast. Snow was still falling outside and it was bitterly cold when an early morning light shafted through the tall windows of The Great Hall.

The news brought by the messenger earlier played on my mind. If Henry had given Hotspur control, it probably implied that he thought he may fail himself, thus he had delegated responsibility and subsequently 'blame' if the need should arise. In reality, our rebellion had only just started and although support was growing rapidly from every corner of Wales, it was not, at this point, well-co-ordinated and this we must do something about. It was imperative that Owain took control completely. If we were not careful, Hotspur would use any lack of co-ordination to his advantage. I decided to talk to Owain later this morning. I had some ideas which would need the help of the Council of Blue Stone to implement successfully.

Chapter Thirteen

"Friends! Please, please—order, order!" the Great Eagle of the Council of Blue Stone appealed for calm but the mayhem in conversation continued, leaving his pleas left unheard. He flapped huge wings, stamped a taloned foot on the branch and screeched loudly. Immediately he started to screech, a dwarf with an enormous belly and large purple nose, picked up the sacred horn and blew three long deep blasts that echoed throughout the chamber. Silence fell in the Council meeting and other than the dripping waterfalls, all was quiet.

Math Fab Mathonwy took his place at the head of the gigantic oak table, he stood erect (well as erect as his ancient aura would allow) and peered down the length of the room at the other members of the Council of Blue Stone. The spirit of the ancient King addressed the anxious waiting throng.

"Friends! We have heard all the news from our member, servant to 'The Prophecy', seer and prophet, Crach Ffinnant. He has brought us news of the rebellion and of progress with the sacred dragon eggs." He fiddled with his ghostly beard. "We are here to serve 'The Prophecy', my friends, and all is now in full flow. We need to address problems, find solutions and give wise counsel to the players in this ancient prophecy."

"We need to send a dragon army to burn the English from the face of the earth!" a goblin chief at the far end of the table shouted, banging his fist into the ancient oak to reinforce his point. "Kill them all!"

"No! No!" the ravens all cawed in unison from a precipice above the table. Carron fluttered from precipice to table and back again in frustration.

"I agree with the ravens," Tan-y-Mynedd spoke up, loudly. His booming voice echoing several times around the cavern.

"Of course you do!" another goblin supported his friend but went a little further. "Lazy and idle they are, laying in caves all day long, only coming out at night, scared of their own shadows!"

"Enough!" Tan-y-Mynedd boomed, his echo loosening rock from the cavern walls which fell, crashing to the ground. The agitated ravens flew from the precipice and circled the table several times before returning to their collective perch. Llwyd ap Crachan Llwyd covered his ears, as did many others.

Math Fab Mathonwy brought his staff down heavily and when it thudded onto the ground, the whole cavern shuddered as if it were a mini earthquake, with sparks of rainbows glistening all around him, he said. "All will have their chance to speak. Now, for the last time, I appeal for order and for sensible discussion and we will have rational orderly discussion. Do you understand?" He thudded the staff onto the ground again with equal effect. "We need to balance our decisions and serve 'The Prophecy', not waste time on our own issues!" He stared intently at both of the goblins. "You goblins are known to be headstrong. This is neither the time nor the place and I urge you to think before you speak."

Both of the goblins looked subdued by his words, but their eyes revealed anger and fire, reflecting the truth. They are, indeed, headstrong. It is one of the reasons why for so many centuries, goblins fell out with everybody they ever had dealings with, as well as each other. What a peculiar folk they can be at times. But, despite this, they held an important seat at the Council of Blue Stone, as did all others who were here, and also some who were not. All is equal in the magical worlds until it is not, and the Council of Blue Stone was no different in this respect.

Once again, Math Fab Mathonwy stood at the head of the table, bringing his staff onto the ground, commanding silence which spread across the huge cavern once more.

"We are aware of all the issues presenting great difficulty and our decision-making must not be biased in any way. It must be fair to all and we must remember, we are duty-bound to serve 'The Prophecy'. Know this, and remember the words therein!" The old King coughed and continued with his speech. "The Dragon Prince will rise in the same year as the ancient dragons themselves, both giving security and hope to their own kind, so 'The Prophecy' states." The old King of Gwynedd shook in his spectral form to further demonstrate his understanding of the words. "It separates the man from the species, does it not?" A murmur of agreement rippled throughout those gathered. "It says both will rise, but sees this as two separate events within the same year. Nowhere in the text, nor in any of the subsequent interpretations, is it stated that the dragons themselves will go to war for the Prince, nor indeed for Wales," concluded Math Fab Mathonwy.

Tan-y-Mynedd was pleased with the words he just heard and spluttered, "I now rest my case!"

Some may have thought he was being sarcastic, but this is not true, it was a fact and one he would not dispute at all. The great dragon had long protested the need to keep away from mankind. I had lost count of the number of times over the years his 'snuff-sneezing' had covered folk in a green dust which instantly sent them to sleep and made them forget ever having seen him and upon waking up several hours later, had a headache akin to a thunderstorm. This method of secrecy, which was used upon those who he had been unable to avoid, worked well for him. I had witnessed this many times myself since I met this great dragon, and that was many decades ago in the mists of time.

I was happy to hear the wise words of the old King. His interpretations were correct and factual.

Tan-y-Mynedd must have heard my thoughts as he suddenly boomed, "And so am I!"

The assembled Council of Blue Stone looked stunned, not understanding his outburst. But I did.

The Elfin leader, with her long silver hair and sharp beautiful features, raised a hand to speak. Math Fab Mathonwy nodded his head, giving silent permission.

She stood and pushed her seat backwards, leaning into the table supported by nimble fingers, bending and bridging elfin hands, coughing to clear her throat, she addressed the Council of Blue Stone. "My friends, please hear my words which are the opinions of my people. We believe this to be wise counsel and share it thus." She flicked her head and cascading hair settled like an avalanche over her narrow shoulders. "The ways of men are well known to all of us in the underworld. It is why there was an 'underworld' to begin with. We, like many of you, were driven here many hundreds of years ago due to the very cruelty we suffered at the hands of man. Now, man is cruel to man. Because we chose our world to be separate and mostly disconnected from man, they can no longer be cruel to us."

The old King gave an all-knowing glance and blinked his acknowledgement for her to continue.

"It is the belief of my people that we must avoid man, unless," she looked stern. "Unless they interfere with us. Yes, we all support 'The Prophecy'. Yes, we all support the Prince and the magical realms are in harmony with all, as they should be! But to pick up the bow is not something we will do. Our arrows must only be used in the defence of our kingdoms."

"This is true for all of us," a dwarf at the other end of the table chipped in.

"Indeed," both goblins asserted.

"Thus, my friends," she continued. "We believe the dragons should not go to war. It is not their war. It is the Prince's war." She looked across at Tan-y-Mynedd and smiling warmly, she added, "Six months ago, your species was at the point of demise and extinction as only three of you still lived. Today, there are many babies and the future is looking secure for generations to come. A war, at this point, would be most destructive. All of the kingdoms must survive." She returned to her seat and drank spring water from a crystal goblet.

Math Fab Mathonwy stood again and acknowledged her contribution. It certainly seemed the Council had reached a conclusion and even though the goblins were happy for Tan-y-Mynedd to spit flame, they themselves would be hiding deep in their own caverns, safely ensconced in ignorance. This is the way of goblins.

I considered for a moment the passing remarks both Owain and Tudur had recently made with regard to 'dragon fire' being a reality. Certainly, they too had made the same assumption as had been made by the Goblins.

Tan-y-Mynedd raised his giant head and sneezed an almighty sneeze up into the cave roof.

CHAPTER FOURTEEN

Carron the Raven alighted on a rock, hopped down onto the grass, skipped down to the water's edge and bending a big black head, dipped his long beak into the icy water and drank deeply for several moments. Thirst now quenched, he lifted a wing and began to preen black silky feathers. Flicking tail feathers, he turned his head all the way around and plucked at them with his beak, first one, then each of the tail feathers in turn. Fluttering wings and waggling his tail, Carron shook his body vigorously, appearing to be a huge black feathery ball, rather than the sleek raven he is. Preening completed, the raven squawked and spreading wings, flew to my shoulder, sticking that sharp beak into my ear again.

"I have grave tidings, Crach," Carron whispered. "Henry has sent Erasmus to The Tower. He has ordered him to contemplate his loyalty to the Crown and told him, in no uncertain terms, he will die there if he does not see sense!"

Poor Erasmus. He was old and frail. I pray this may not be too much for him. This is, indeed, very grave news.

Whilst at the council of Blue Stone, time had allowed some discussion with Llwyd ap Crachan Llwyd, my old Master. He had already heard about Erasmus seeking solitude at Glastonbury and that he was then hunted by the King and arrested, which was bad enough, but I wondered if he knew about this latest bad news. He remarked that he felt Erasmus may not survive the King's wrath and frankly, neither did I, especially now.

Even from the spirit world, my Master was serving 'The Prophecy', as were so many others. Some realised they were servants to 'The Prophecy', some did not. There was no doubt that things were becoming volatile. The rebellion was rapidly evolving into a full-scale war. My Master told me that within twelve months, all would unite under Glyndwr's banner from every corner of Wales and many surprises were yet in store. He sensed no dark clouds at the moment but all these things can change very quickly, just like the weather.

Interrupting my thoughts, Carron spoke again. "There is much more to tell, Crach, as the Raven Kingdom is falling out with itself."

"What do you mean?" I asked. "Falling out with itself?"

Carron hopped onto my other shoulder and continued, "As you know, many of us live in small groups and some of us serve the magical realm. The splintering of opinions are like poisoned daggers. As the point imbeds, the poison spreads. Ravens from the King's Tower are very upset and rebellious over the arrest of Erasmus. He is their wizard and seer. They are not loyal to the Crown but they are loyal to Erasmus."

Erasmus had been wizard and seer to the Royal Court for over six decades. The fact that he had served the kingdom and its regents well has never been beyond doubt, and certainly not questioned by those of us who know him. Henry had ignored advice from Erasmus to avoid conflict with Owain, and also ignored his counsel against defrauding Owain of gold and of land. He then ignored his pleas, and, moreover, ignored his word. Henry being Henry, had not listened at all and went ahead with his ill-thought-out actions. The result, of course, is the mayhem we now find ourselves a part of. Erasmus left the King's castle in the dead of night and travelled to Glastonbury to a monastery but now Henry has imprisoned the old wizard in The Tower after dragging him halfway around the country in chains.

"The ravens are loyal to Erasmus, Crach. They see him imprisoned in The Tower, helpless to be able to work towards peace. The ravens will rebel and seek like-minded others!" he squawked and pecked at my ear in agitation.

"Do you think others will join you, Carron?" I asked.

"They are already saying as much, Crach," he bristled the feathers around his neck and continued. "We all know Erasmus will not give in to the King and although Henry may not send him to the block, he will let him rot in The Tower. Therefore, it is a forgone conclusion they will join us."

He flew down to the ground to peck here and there, as ravens do.

I hoped that Erasmus would survive but Henry had committed a grave mistake by imprisoning the old wizard in The Tower. As a consequence, Henry was now in danger of completely losing the sources of any magic he may still have left within his Kingdom. If Erasmus were to die, the ravens would surely abandon Henry as he no longer had a wizard serving in his Court. If they were to abandon Henry, they would take with them any possibility of him being able to use any magic and for the first time in history, there would be no ravens serving the English Crown. This, indeed, was a travesty Henry was ignorant of.

Carron announced his imminent departure and immediately took flight, heading northwards. I watched him until he was but a tiny black dot in the sky, before disappearing altogether.

My mind would not rid itself of thoughts of Erasmus. As I wandered down the valley along the drovers' path, the sun began to burst through a dark grey sky. Perhaps I had been given two omens. One, the loss of all magical links to the English throne and, two, although the darkness surrounding Erasmus was real, perhaps the sun shows light to ease his suffering. Time would tell.

***

The stone walls were damp and the candle on the table offered no warmth to the body sat hunched on a battered old chair next to it. Rainwater, leaking in at a small window, formed a pool on the floor where it soaked into the already dampened straw. Next to the candle on the table, sat a wooden jug and cup, empty of anything thirst-quenching, now invaded by a cockroach or two.

The blanket over the old man's shoulders had seen better days, being threadbare and worn, enabling no real warmth. His hair was long, grey and greasy, hanging in clumps down slumped shoulders and back. Here was a man whose life hung by a thread.

Suddenly, a huge lock was removed from the door with a crash and a bolt pulled across noisily. As the door opened, the old man raised his head to see the King standing in front of him in all his finery. Two soldiers stood behind the King with not a smile between them.

The King stared down at the old man with no hint of compassion for this aged wizard who had always served the monarchy to the best of his abilities. Henry told the guards to bring him a stool and then to leave them, a command to which they promptly complied.

With the door closed behind them, Henry sat on the stool and the old man watched his every move through eyes weary with age and pain.

"Well, look at you now, Erasmus! This is what happens when you betray your King. Did you ever think I would just forget your betrayal and let you disappear? Do you realise how you have offended your King, Wizard? And where is your magic now?" mocked Henry.

Erasmus was cold and knew he had a chill. No food had passed his lips in four days. He felt weak and, in his soul, he wished for a way out of this dreadful predicament, although he had believed for some months his end was in sight. '*Was this to be his end?*' he wondered as he stared at Henry.

Henry continued to berate the old man. "You have no words for your King, Wizard?" Henry banged his fist on the table, knocking the empty jug and cup to the floor. "Not as comfortable here as your quarters at the Court, is it? You must wish you were able to sit by your fire and eat a hearty meal?" Still, the old man said nothing. "Answer your King, damn you!" Henry shouted, crashing his fist into the table again.

Erasmus coughed quietly, even trying to breathe quietly in an attempt to remain as silent as he could.

"The damp is on your chest, old man!" Henry laughed.

"Is that why you don't speak?"

"What would be the point?" the old man whispered.

"What was that?" Henry sat back. "You spoke! What did you say?"

Erasmus straightened his posture as much as his age and decrepitude would allow, feeling the damp seeping into his weary bones. Flicking dirty hair from his face with gnarled fingers, Erasmus looked at the King intently and as he did so, the old man's eyes became bright, twinkling in the candlelight.

"There is no point in me speaking as my words are of no importance to you," Erasmus continued. "I cannot think of one prediction, of one casting of runes or of one piece of wisdom I have ever given to you that you have ever truly accepted. Surely, Your Highness, even you must understand. Words cast in air are but that. And at my age, 'air' is a precious commodity not to be wasted."

"You dare to mock your King, Wizard?" Henry was on the verge of rage and even now he continued to ignore the words of his wizard.

"I speak only the truth, which is the reason for my silence. I have nothing to say to you that I have not said before. I am an old man so there is nothing you can do to me that the years have not done already."

Henry stood and kicked the stool away in temper. He drew his dagger from his belt and stuck it into the table with brute force.

"I could cut your throat!" Henry leaned menacingly over the table.

Erasmus shrugged his shoulders and whispered, "Your Majesty will be doing me a favour by ending my misery. You will do your worst in any event, without prompting from me or any other."

Henry was furious and close to exploding. His shouting brought the guards to the door to see what the commotion was all about, one of them entering the cell in case his service was required but as soon as the door opened, Henry turned on his heel and stormed out, barging past both guards with curses on his lips. Closing and locking the door behind them, the guards followed the King.

Erasmus slumped over the table, his head resting on folded arms. The old man avoided sleep because dreams were invaded by nightmares as, indeed, were his waking hours. He tried to think of something to warm his thoughts and heart and allowed his mind to drift to Glastonbury and the peace he had briefly known there.

CHAPTER FIFTEEN

Essex felt somewhat better now he was returned to London. All this cavorting about, preparing for war, was a little tiresome these days. A seasoned warrior he may be, but even Essex thought he was getting too old for battle and was certainly against giving his life for a King who cared for nobody but his own being. In the near two years Henry had held the throne, nothing but problem after trouble occurred. From bringing austerity to his Kingdom to insulting his knights of the realm, bringing war with Scotland and now with Wales, his reign thus far had been a catalogue of nightmares for all to behold. In his heart, Essex despaired for the future. Henry just had no moral compass and led his life with no consideration for others. Essex had witnessed Henry's imprisonment and subsequent murder of Richard II as had others, but all were quite powerless to do anything about it.

Essex had suffered a hard ride back from Wales, with the weather most inclement for the whole journey. Stopping off in Shrewsbury for a couple of days to visit friends, he took every advantage of taking a small break before returning to Court. Now he was here, awaiting the King's pleasure. He was stirred from his thoughts as the door opened and a soldier entered.

"My Lord," he announced. "The King will see you now."

"Thank you," Essex replied, getting up from his seat, following the soldier to King Henry's chambers. As soon as Essex came into the room he was greeted by the King.

"So, Essex, you are back," Henry smiled.

"It warms my heart to see you well, my King," Essex said, returning the smile.

"And what of Wales and its devilish weather? I hate that country nearly as much as I hate every Welshman, especially Glyndwr!" The King poured himself a goblet of wine.

"Yes, my Lord." Essex looked out of the window, trying to put himself in another place. It was one of the ways he had found he could remove himself partially from the King's words which, nowadays, he found tiresome in the extreme.

"Something taking your fancy, Essex?" Henry asked. "Does something outside concern you more than inside? Inside with your King!"

"No, my Lord, I simply glanced. I meant no offence." Essex bowed his head in submission.

"Very well," Henry conceded with a cursory wave of his hand, inviting Essex to take a seat.

"Thank you, my Lord." Essex took the chair and averted his gaze from the window.

"And so, Essex, I have dispatched Hotspur to Wales to

organise the rabble it has become. He has my royal permission to do what he will to bring this rebellion to nothing but smoke. I will have Glyndwr and all his accomplices in The Tower. Every one of them!" Henry poured more wine. "I already hold Erasmus in The Tower."

This was news to Essex, he had no idea and showed surprise at hearing about the old man's incarceration. He felt the King's action was both cruel and unjust but knew better than to express his opinion. But he was pleased he had given Hotspur the position of dealing with Wales rather than himself as he was a much younger man and as far as he was concerned, he could have the job and be welcome to it. Perhaps he may be able to slide away and quietly retire from the King's service, although he knew there would be little chance of that in the months to come.

Henry took a large gulp of wine, belched, and called for food. Within next to no time, the court servants covered the table with a repast fit for five men.

"Eat with me, Essex. Your King commands it. I hate to eat alone!" he ordered as he gulped yet more wine.

Essex tore some ham from the hock and used bread as a trencher. A mint and mustard sauce added tang. It was his favourite meal. He thought the ham was extremely tender as a piece melted in his mouth.

"Good, Essex?" Henry enquired.

Given Essex had his mouth full of bread and ham, he merely nodded his head politely.

Henry ripped a leg from a chicken on a platter and proceeded to devour it to the bone. The royal wolfhounds would eat well this night.

Few words were exchanged between Essex and the King as they both ate heartily. The food on the table slowly disappeared into the mouths of the two men. Essex sipped at the wine and Henry called for another flagon. With the food all but gone, the servants cleared the table, returning with fruit and two more flagons of wine. '*Someone was thinking on their feet this night.*' Essex thought. If Henry drank both, he would be sure to fall asleep, thus the servants could have the rest of the night to themselves. Essex smiled to himself. Henry poured himself more wine and taking his dagger, he stabbed at an apple in the fruit bowl.

Essex waited for the King to speak but he seemed content with silence, for the time being, a source of great relief to him under the circumstances when conversation was difficult and fraught with hidden agenda.

Henry was becoming very sleepy, his vision seemed far away and as Essex watched the King out of the corner of his eye, he thought he may nod off and he would be able to go to bed. Although, on reflection, he dare not leave unless dismissed by the King and if he failed to do so before he fell asleep, Essex would have to sit on this hard chair until Henry woke, which was not a pleasant prospect. He coughed loudly and successfully jerked Henry back into consciousness.

"Ah, Essex," he said. "I think your King may retire. Tomorrow, we will talk more. So, I bid you a goodnight." Henry called for his page.

Essex heaved a sigh of relief and wished the King a good night. Considering Henry's mood, Essex thought the evening had gone reasonably well. Henry had not insulted him too much, few words had actually been exchanged between them and he had eaten a grand meal. The warmth of his cot awaited.

As the cock crowed at dawn, Henry awoke feeling quite good for a change. Even though he had supped an inordinate volume of wine the night before, there was no hangover for him today. He called for his page and dressed before breaking his fast. Fruit, bread and ham filled an empty royal stomach and he belched several times after quaffing a goblet of ale. It was still only seven in the morning, but given that Henry was up early and ready for business, he could see little reason why everybody else should not feel the same.

He summoned Lord Essex. "Good morning, My Lord," Essex announced as he entered the King's chambers. He bowed his head, as was expected of him.

Henry raised his head from the desk and pushed a parchment aside, replacing the quill into the inkwell. "Essex, your King is in good spirits this morning and so a good morning to you also. Now sit, and let us proceed to matters of importance." Ordered Henry.

Essex sat, as commanded, but found himself staring out of the window. Remembering Henry's bitter reaction the previous evening, Essex quickly averted his attention to the King's presence.

"So, Essex. Firstly, I wish to discuss what I will do about Erasmus, it worries me greatly. I was very angry with him yesterday and could have easily slit his throat." Henry paused.

"My Lord, he is an old man and has served the Court for decades," Essex chipped in but spoke quietly, not wishing to disturb the King's good mood.

"He betrayed me, Essex. He left without a word," Henry's words faded off and he started to fiddle with the quill.

"My Lord, he may have abandoned the Court but I do not think he betrayed you," Essex continued to speak quietly.

"I feel betrayed, Essex. I do feel betrayed," he continued to fiddle with the quill.

Essex made no comment but thought to himself. '*Well, you never did listen to him and you ignored all his warnings.*

You made him feel superfluous.' As the silence continued, Henry fiddled with his quill and Essex had another thought. *'Now you know what Glyndwr must feel like and there is no comparison to be drawn between the two alleged betrayals in their purest definitions.'* He could never voice his words to Henry as a rage would be assured, with his actions becoming most unpredictable.

Henry broke the silence. "I think I should bring the Erasmus matter to an end!"

"An end, My Lord?" Essex queried.

"Yes, Essex. An end!" He placed the quill on the table and ran his finger along the feather, smiling to himself. Henry raised his head. "I have three options, Essex, and one of them must be decided upon this day. I will have no more of this!"

"Yes, My Lord." Essex sounded pensive.

"I can free him, giving him a pardon so he can disappear into retirement." Henry picked up a goblet and poured himself some ale.

"That would be a kind act, My Lord." Essex felt hopeful.

"Or!" Henry continued. "I can let him rot in that cell. He won't last long."

"My Lord, do you really think that would satisfy you?" Essex attempted to plead to Henry's kinder side, although he was not sure if he had one. "Or!" Henry completed with his last option. "I can have his head!"

Essex was mortified. "My Lord, this would be both a pointless and meaningless death. Please! What good would this serve?"

"It would serve to free me, Essex. Once and for all!"

A raven squawked in anger from outside the King's chambers. Its call answered by others.

Essex shuddered.

CHAPTER SIXTEEN

F og and mist rolled down the valley, a sheet of rain fell like a screen in front of my eyes. Soaked through to the skin, I was a very uncomfortable dwarf. Cwtch, my horse, shared in my misery of this inclemency. Would it never stop raining?

Together with Owain and Tudur, we ambled down the valley on our mounts but it was hard to see five paces in front as the mist was so thick. Wolf, my canine friend had returned from venturing in the high mountains and forests. It had been some time since we had seen each other and it was good to have him back, lolloping at my side again as I rode. He too was soaked through, his thick coat sodden. He stopped and shook periodically to free himself of excessive raindrops.

We rode ahead of a troop numbering thirty of Owain's seasoned warriors. Emrys, Moelwyn and Griff followed Tudur, with Emrys holding the dragon's banner drooping dismally in the dampness. The rain started to ease and the mist began to lift but within ten minutes, it rolled in again. I ached for it to go and for the sun to shine but instead, the light rain turned into another downpour and the clouds rolled back into the valley. Our little band rode on.

Wolf had gone on ahead of us and I saw him returning through the mist, looking anxious. We could not see far but he seemed to have sensed something was there. His ruff rose and his back bristled as this great wolf let out a low growl. We all stopped in our tracks and stood silently, as shadows within the mist. Hands moved to sword hilts. Owain raised an arm, motioning silently for all to remain perfectly still and be as quiet as mice. We stood like ghosts when out of the mist two riders appeared. Upon seeing the banner of the dragon, they tried to turn their mounts around but Moelwyn and Griff were on them in a flash. Griff knocked one of the riders from his horse and he fell heavily to the ground. Moelwyn took the other by grabbing the reins of his steed as it reared up and pranced on the spot, throwing up rocks and mud. Tudur's sword was at the rider's throat.

"English!" Tudur broke the silence. "English, Brother!"

The Englishman, who now lay prostrate on the wet ground, wore a satchel which had sprung open as he fell. Several sealed parchments lay scattered in the mud around him. Tudur jumped from his horse and gathered them up.

"Messengers, Brother!" Tudur announced.

"Bind these men to their horses, Emrys!" commanded Owain.

"Why not just kill them?" Tudur asked.

"Because they may prove to be useful," I interjected.

"And I would have questions for them," added Owain.

The rain eased but the mist drifted in once more, although occasionally the sun managed to break through the dark clouds. I appreciated the warmth as we rode on with the sky becoming clearer as the wind high above us spurred clouds on a journey to who knows where.

The weather continued to improve as our journey progressed, becoming quite warm in the clearing sky. With the aid of the late winter sun and a fresh breeze, I was beginning to dry out a little.

We were still half a day's ride from Llangollen where Valle Crucis Abbey was situated. Owain had a meeting arranged with the Abbot to discuss the support of the Cistercians in the uprising. He would question the prisoners later to see if they knew anything more about the dispatches they carried for the King. Tudur opened one of them, breaking the wax seal which bore the arms of the King's agent. "It is from Hotspur. These are letters to the King!"

"Most fortunate," I said

"And the letter says what, Tudur?" Owain asked his brother.

Tudur scanned the rich script written in black ink on yellow parchment, the signature being that of Hotspur. "He tells of receiving the King's commands. He says that rewards will be posted to encourage others to betray you!" He read out loud, before passing the message to Owain.

"Nobody would dare do that!" exclaimed Emrys

"Not a Welshman, anyway!" piped up Moelwyn.

"Only those with a death wish," added Tudur.

Owain stopped reading the manuscript and refolding it, secreted the letter inside his tunic.

"I will keep this one, for now, Tudur. We will look at the others when we reach the Abbey."

Tudur threw the satchel over his shoulder whilst Moelwyn and Griff tied the soldiers to their horses.

Owain looked up at the sun and felt the warmth on his face. Suddenly, he dug his heels into his mount, it reared up and took off at the gallop, its hooves biting into the soft earth. Tudur signalled we should all follow at speed and in silence. Coming to the end of the valley, I could see the outline of the Abbey silhouetted in the distance against the afternoon sun. We could be there in less than half an hour.

As Glyndwr's retinue of seasoned warriors trotted through the Abbey gates, the monks hurried here and there, preparing for the visit of the Prince of Wales. Owain had been here many times in the past but this was his first visit as Prince. The Abbot stood on the steps of the chapel and hailed a wave as we rode in, stepping down the stairs, he rushed across the courtyard to meet us with his cassock billowing in the wind.

"Prince Owain! Welcome to our Abbey. And, Crach Ffinnant, I bid you a warm welcome too. Is that Tudur Glyndwr I see before me? How the heavens have blessed us!"

The Abbot took hold of Cwtch's reins and she began to prance on the spot, resenting the restraint.

"Crach. How good it is to see you. In fact, to see you all. There is food and ale for your men, my Prince," he hailed a passing monk and instructed him to escort Emrys and the others to the kitchens. Emrys quickly gathered the hungry men behind him and led them off to eat. Other monks and lay brothers stabled our horses, filling a nosebag for each of them.

"Gentlemen!" the Abbot announced. "Let us dine together while we discuss the state of our nation."

"A wise choice of discussion," said Owain, smiling.

"I'm starving!" Tudur exclaimed as he walked briskly

behind the Abbot and Owain. I brought up the rear, limping a little as my leg was stiff from so many hours spent in the saddle. I was not as young as I used to be. We followed the Abbot across the courtyard and climbed the steps into the apartments.

The Cistercians were a much-disciplined Order and had been in Wales for over two hundred years, since before the year 1200. The monks performed religious duties as well as illustrating their beautiful books and managing the lay brothers, who did most of the real work in keeping the Abbey self-sufficient.

The Abbot's quarters were not luxurious as such but they were very comfortable. A large oval table sat in the centre of the room with several high-backed chairs around it. To one end was his desk, with parchments stacked high upon it. A box shaped like a small coffin also sat on the desk. He told us it contained the relic of a famous saint but he never did tell us who or what it was. One wall was lined with shelves, stacked with volumes of books on many subjects, all lovingly illustrated by the monks. At the opposite end of the room to his desk was a private chapel.

"Gentlemen, please sit and make yourselves comfortable. It is time to rest after your long ride." He gestured toward the chairs at the table where we three weary travellers sat down.

With the prisoners secure under guard in the stable, any questioning of them could wait until later.

"I will look at those letters now, Tudur, if you please?" Owain sat and waited while his brother removed the satchel from his back and opened it. He dug deep, taking hold of the letters and passing them to Owain.

"Thank you, Tudur," Owain said as he began to open one of the letters, breaking the seal with a snap. He read the contents and smiling, passed it on to me. "Read that, Crach!"

I took the letter and began to read. The script was by an educated hand but it was not that of Hotspur it was from the hand of Lord Edmund. Surprise of surprises, I thought to myself. Now I could see why Owain had smiled. Here, in my grasp, I held his report to the King of his futile search for the dragons. I read the words with keen interest, as had Owain.

"So, he has searched high and low to no avail as nobody knew of any such living creature. He goes on to say he is at the butt end of people's mockery and has become a laughing stock, far and wide." I chuckled under my breath at the mere thought. "He bids the King to allow him to return to Court!"

"I bet he does!" Tudur chipped in whilst pouring himself a glass of wine.

The Abbot had fine glasses from France, drinking vessels reserved for special visitors. I suppose a visiting Welsh Prince qualifies for their use and this was a special occasion after all.

As we settled down to read the full contents of the satchel, the Abbot organised food and more wine. The table was soon laden with all sorts of delicacies, served by two lay brothers who scurried back and forth through a secret door in the wall. I say 'secret' because it did not look like a door in the traditional sense, it just seemed like a part of the wall but every now and then, as the lay brothers entered with more trays of food, the wall simply opened! A large fire blazed and the room soon warmed, airing our damp clothes. With the table fully covered with food and drink, the Abbot sat down and invited us to pray before we ate.

Fresh trout, poached on a trencher, together with an almond and garlic sauce, surrounded by fresh cabbage and watercress, lay steaming on a silver platter in the centre of the table. Freshly baked bread from the Abbey bakery, still warm from the oven, along with two legs of roasted lamb accompanied by mint jelly, surrounded the trout.

Prayers said the Abbot announced. "I would now like to formally welcome you to our Abbey, my Prince." The Abbot prepared a toast and we all raised our fine glasses to Owain Glyndwr, Prince of Wales. "Now, please eat, my friends— eat!"

"Well," Owain began, with a piece of lamb between his fingers. "This is a feast fit for a king. I thank you, Abbot."

"You are all most welcome. More wine?" he offered, passing the elegantly engraved glass carafe, full of deep red and sweet wine made from the grapes grown in the Abbey's vineyard. Fruit from their orchard, apples, pears, crab-apples made into jelly, also adorned the table. A grand feast indeed.

We all ate heartily. Especially Tudur, who managed two fair-sized trout as well as a healthy portion of lamb, not to mention spoonfuls of crab-apple jelly! I hoped his tummy would not complain too much later this evening or, indeed, tomorrow morning.

"All this war work makes a man very hungry!" Tudur explained between mouthfuls of tender lamb.

Owain raised his eyebrows, smiled and took a large bite from a ripe pear. I had eaten more than enough and the two glasses of wine I enjoyed with the meal, made me feel quite sleepy. The lay brothers re-appeared and cleared away the empty platters. Tudur sat back in his chair and yawned deeply. "I am weary, Brother. It has certainly been a long day."

"It has," I agreed. "This dwarf is almost ready for his sheepskins."

"I thought we may talk further," Owain said to the Abbot, who had also eaten an enormous amount. He too yawned from the effects of the good food and wine.

"Very well. I can take a hint. It seems as I am outvoted." Owain looked at our heavy eyelids. The Abbot's chin rested on his chest, even he had begun to nod off!

"So, to bed, my friends," Owain said, dismissing the rest of the day. "Tomorrow will come soon enough."

The Abbot instructed a lay brother to show us to our sleeping quarters for the night and bade us all 'good dreams by God's grace'.

Owain and Tudur shared a room in the Prior's quarters, whilst I was given a cell in the monks' dormitory. It was not long before I fell asleep with a full tummy under the warmth of sheepskins. At that moment, I felt very content.

I slept soundly for some hours and although I did dream, I could not recall anything when I woke. Perhaps the wine dulled my ability to remember or maybe I was overtired. Still, it made a nice change for me to enjoy a solid sleep without disturbance. I smiled to myself, making the most of the temporary respite from invasive dreamscapes.

I took breakfast the next morning in the dining room, sitting at a vacant part of a bench between two monks. Porridge and bread were plentiful but I only ate one small bowl of porridge as my stomach was still content from last evening's feast. I did drink plenty of spring water though, needing to rinse away the effects of the wine I had enjoyed. Just as I was draining my second jug of water, Tudur walked through the door and upon catching sight of me, he made a beeline to where I sat, taking the bench opposite.

"Good morning, Crach!" Tudur beamed, none the worse for wear from his excesses of the previous night.

"Shush!" the monk next to me scowled, reminding us that food was always taken in silence in the dining room. Tudur looked mildly embarrassed but he smiled and silently helped himself to some bread and honey. The silent contemplative monk glared at Tudur, having perceived his sarcasm, light in spirit though it may have been. Having finished his breakfast, the monk quietly stood, gathered his bowl, spoon, and mug and left the bench. Tudur turned to me and gave a knowing smile, which I returned, unseen by the monk who was now leaving his utensils by the door. I personally think silence is a wonderful thing, unlike others I could mention!

The door re-opened and a monk rushed in. He hurried over to where Tudur and I sat, bent into Tudur's ear and whispered. Tudur then looked at me and leaned over the table, touching my arm gently with his finger, attracting my attention fully. With a flick of his head towards the door, he gestured we needed to leave—which we did, quietly!

I noticed it was a fine morning as we walked across the courtyard. The cock had only just crowed but many of the monks were long from their beds, busying themselves with daily tasks.

We followed the monk into the Abbot's apartment where we found Owain and the Abbot breakfasting together. Owain swallowed a piece of fruit and bade us both a good morning. We joined them at the table and the Abbot invited us to eat. I declined, whilst Tudur helped himself to some ham and bread. I did request spring water though and the Abbot passed me the jug.

"And so, let us talk!" Owain requested as he put down his goblet and rested his elbows on the table, propping his chin on cradled fingers. "The Abbot and I have spoken at length and there are concerns that we have not yet considered. We need plans to prevent any unwanted surprises! I think you will all agree."

We all silently nodded in agreement.

Owain continued, "The Abbot has informed me there are fears amongst the Cistercians. Some are loyal to the throne through the Royal Charter only, but is that enough to be able to maintain loyalty? Loyalties are becoming divided but it seems to be for personal, not national, gain. I am in gloom at such paths being taken. This is Wales, thus all should be loyal to our country, crown or no crown." Owain was becoming upset. This did not happen very often but Wales was in his bloodline and he would have her freedom from the tyranny of the English.

Chapter Seventeen

Four lay brothers sat outside the stable in the early morning sun.

"It seems as if the rain will stay away today," a brother of slight stature with sharp features and a large hairy wart on his chin suggested.

"Oh, I do hope so, William. I am fed up with getting wet day after day. We never really get a chance to dry out, do we?" Timothy responded. He was the eldest of the brothers, in his fiftieth year, with the wrinkles of life written on his chubby face. His tonsure was silver and his face the colour of wild strawberries. Whiskers sprouted from his round chin. "Apart from the discomfort of wet weather, there comes a time in a man's life when retirement is most appealing. There would be no more rising in all weathers before the cock crows. No more blistered hands from chopping wood. I now have pain in all sorts of places and a stiffness in my knees and elbows beyond description," he sighed.

William nodded in silent sympathy, although he was considerably younger than Timothy and really had little idea of the discomfort his fellow lay brother complained about. When you are young, old age seems so far off until one morning, you wake to find it has arrived with the dawn.

"He doesn't know what you're on about. I wouldn't waste my time trying to explain," said Silas, who was not much younger than Timothy so knew exactly what he meant. Silas was still strong but only in his physical body. Thick muscular forearms poked from the sleeves of his habit and strong hands toyed with a pruning knife, carving a small piece of wood into a tiny cross. Sadly, Silas had experienced a lot of unhappiness in his life and was now a depressed soul, rapidly becoming devoid of spirit. He had no enthusiasm for anything nowadays. Silas related all other's suffering as equal to his own. It was even quite rare for him to speak at all these days. Timothy must have struck a chord.

The fourth member of this small band of lay brothers flicked a pebble at Silas. "Cheer up, you old goat, you are not dead yet!" Ewan laughed. He was one of the youngest of the lay brothers and one of the tallest. He had only been at the Abbey for five years and at fifteen, he towered above all. He certainly was a giant to me, although he was incredibly thin with the face of a much older person. Perhaps working outside in all weathers was seasoning his face, just as it had with Timothy. Ewan squatted and playfully tossed small stones into a bucket of water standing by the stable door. With cheekbones high, eyes bold and bright, he still held the enthusiasm and ignorance of youth.

I left Owain and Tudur discussing the other letters which had been intercepted on their passage to the King. Of course, I knew the content of two of them. One announced rewards from Hotspur for the capture of Glyndwr and his followers. He awaited the King's response but it had yet to be delivered, if, indeed, it should still be. The second contained Lord Edmund's account of his search for the dragons and pleas, requesting he give up his quest and return to Court. I would wait to hear of the other letters later. Fresh air was the order of the morning for me. Spring water had cleansed my blood of the wine but now I needed fresh air to fully revitalise me. As I walked towards the small group of lay brothers, I took a deep breath but my lungs protested slightly as the cold air caught them.

Timothy knew me from my many visits over the years and hailed cheerfully as I approached. "Morning, Master Crach! It is a fine day."

"It is Brother Timothy—well, for the moment anyway," I replied.

Upon reaching the stables, I glanced through the window at the two English soldiers chained in an empty stall, depriving a horse of its bed. Both slept and, surprisingly, had developed no further bruising. They still had to be questioned, but it would have to wait until Tudur completed his deliberations with Owain and the Abbot.

Silas saw me glance at the prisoners and remarked, "Be they to die, Master Crach?"

"Best thing really!" said Ewan, who was too young to know any better.

"Not always," Timothy said, looking at me with quizzical eyes.

"Quite right," I agreed. "A dead man cannot talk and

there may be messages he has yet to deliver."

"I still think they would be better dead," Ewan added. "Bloody English!"

"You are English, Ewan!" Silas interjected.

"No, I'm not!" he said in his own defence.

"You are!" Brother Timothy added.

"Not!" Ewan was adamant.

"You were born in Chester," William affirmed.

"Wasn't!" Ewan dug his heels in.

"You were, Ewan, and that's an end to the matter!" William asserted his superiority by age if nothing else.

Ewan looked glum and stared at the ground, twitching nervously.

I pondered a question for Ewan and decided to pose it. "Tell me, Ewan. Why would an Englishman be happy to see his fellows killed?"

"I do not know them," Ewan protested.

"Exactly," said, Timothy. "You don't know them."

"I know I do not want to be English," Ewan muttered under his breath.

"What was that?" I asked gently.

"I do not want to be English!" This time he shouted and almost stamped his foot like a small child in deference to a parent's command.

Timothy put his hand out to Ewan and invited him to sit. Silas urged him to calm down by putting a silent finger to pursed lips, inviting him to be quiet.

"I am English," said Silas. "But I can't say as I am proud to be so."

"Yes, but you don't wish them dead, do you?" William asked.

"No, of course not," Silas smiled. "I do not wish anyone

dead. I abhor violence of any kind."

I agreed wholeheartedly with this.

"We are having great problems, Crach. The monasteries at Cym and Strata Florida are under great pressure from the King to disassociate themselves from your Prince and the rebellion," he stuttered, more from anxiety than from a speech impediment. "Our Chapters are faced with division from both within our walls and without. Many of our brothers support the rebellion but some of the Priors and others are afraid they will lose the Royal Charter. There is also a rumour Henry will order his soldiers to take over the monasteries and evict anyone who is loyal to Prince Owain."

"You have heard many things that I have not!" I said, surprised by his words, although I did know much of the relationship between the Cistercians and the Crown. For over two hundred years they had forged civilisation from rock and forest, bringing their skills as farmers, builders, and innovators to Wales. Most of the abbeys were self-sufficient in all they needed and were places of hard work, learning and prayer. Therefore, it is hardly surprising that the Cistercians became immersed in Welsh life and all that may bring. But now it has brought division. For the Cistercians, this was a hard place to be and I am sure those who may be serving the Crown, do so as a matter of practical politics rather than anything else.

The Cistercians were, by Royal Charter, tax collectors for the Crown and over the last few years, heavier taxation, the disintegration of our economy and increased friction between the Welsh and the English Lords had grown by the day. The Cistercians must soon decide whose side they are on and this decision could come more quickly than may be expected.

"These are times of great concern to us, Crach," Timothy said looking anxious. "Be we Welsh or English, we are firstly, and lastly, Cistercians."

"Of that, there is no doubt," I agreed. "And you have to do as your masters direct as, indeed, must we all."

Timothy stood and shook straw from his cassock. "This is not just a rebellion is it, Crach? This is a war. Where will it end?"

I held his arm to offer some reassurance. "Well, Timothy, it has only just begun so as to where it will end, I have no answer for you, I am afraid. None at all."

"We understand, Master Crach." William stood up, with a little assistance from Ewan, who still looked rather frightened. "Well, brothers, we must go to our work before the Prior kicks our backsides."

All four of the lay brothers were now on their feet and bade me farewell as they went about their duties. I sat on a mound of straw with my back against the stable wall and did something I have not done in a long while, I lit my pipe and had a long relaxing smoke of wormwood.

CHAPTER EIGHTEEN

Tudur and Owain wandered slowly across the courtyard, deep in conversation with the Abbot. I took a great draw on my pipe and exhaled a long plume of smoke.

"Ah, Crach!" Tudur called. "We would have a word with the prisoners now."

I turned around and looked into the window. "They are asleep!" I shared my observation.

"Not for long!" Tudur replied, striding towards the stable door with renewed purpose in his step. "I will soon have them awake!" He marched through the door, crashing it open and gave the prisoners a sharp kick each on the thigh, from which they immediately woke with cries of pain.

"Hold fast, Tudur!" Owain stemmed his brother's flow. "Remember what we just agreed?"

"I am sorry, Brother!" Tudur backed away from the two Englishman who were lying prostrate with thighs stinging as bruising emerged. "I got carried away."

"Yes, you did, didn't you?" Owain edgily agreed. "And not for the first time either."

"And it is not likely to be the last," Tudur laughed.

I was certain it would not be the last time. Tudur was very quick to act, often before he gave any thought to his actions, unlike Owain, who was quite the opposite in manner and make-up.

Owain ordered two of his men to feed the prisoners and then bring them over to the paddock, ready for riding.

"Ready to ride?" I questioned with surprise.

"We have read their letters and decided to let Henry receive them, but not before we have tampered with them a little," Owain whispered to me.

"And, perhaps, make a few alterations and even additions," the Abbot quietly chipped in.

"Yes, this will be fun, Crach," Tudur laughed loudly, as we all did.

Whilst the prisoners ate breakfast and prepared to continue on their journey, we four wandered over towards the lake. I wondered if the ghost of Septimus Tupp might be listening.

"This is a wise idea, My Lord," I said as we walked along the path with our feet crunching on the gravel beneath us. "I assume one of the monks will use his skills as an illustrator to assist us in this task."

"You assume correctly, Crach," Owain confirmed.

The Abbot tapped my shoulder and said, "We decided to let Hotspur's letter go as it is. On reflection, not to do so would only postpone the inevitable. It will be better to let them get on with whatever they must do, and do their worst. We have gone too far now, so no harm can be done, other than what already has been."

As we reached the lakeside, I said, "I believe, My Lord, that Hotspur will turn tail on Henry. I have seen it in my runes and it will not be too long before he does. So, I agree, no purpose will be served by preventing the delivery of his letter. It would disturb the natural flow of things." I stopped momentarily to massage the calf on my right leg, still aching with cramp from yesterday's hard ride.

"Are you in pain?" asked the Abbot with genuine concern.

"He is," Owain confirmed.

"But too proud to admit it. Eh, Crach?" Tudur chuckled, prodding me humorously in the ribs.

"I am in some discomfort," I admitted. "But it will soon pass."

"And what of the other letters?" I asked.

"There are three others," Tudur replied.

"Yes, three, Crach!" Owain looked very pleased with himself. "As with the Hotspur letter, we will not alter Lord Edmund's report, it speaks on its own of his crass behaviour. It will be a good thing for Henry to learn the truth."

"But the others are different," he smiled, knowingly. "One tells of troop placements and proposed movements. This will be copied for us, but altered for Henry's eyes. We will change dates, times and places which will confuse his plans to liaise with his Lords."

"Another lists supplies held at Conwy Castle. We will alter this to reflect a need for refurbishment of arms and food and then, when the supplies arrive, our cousins from Anglesey can take the castle."

"The final letter gives information about the money taken

in taxation which has been collected and lays underground at Hotspur's castle, awaiting delivery to London and the King's coffers. It suggests dates for transportation." Owain paused and was interrupted by Tudur.

"And we will take it!"

"This is, indeed, a good plan." I felt quite excited by the ingenuity of such deceit. "But, of course, the riders may tell Henry they had been captured, thus he may suspect the letters were opened and the information now known by the enemy. Or maybe not. I have an idea which may prevent Henry from suspecting a thing, but it would take one of the riders to swear allegiance to you, my Lord."

"Carry on, Crach," Owain urged as he leaned against a tree, looking more relaxed.

"Yes, please do, Crach. I am intrigued," the Abbot knelt to listen, as did Tudur.

"Well, if one of them returns with a story of being ambushed by our soldiers, saying he only just managed to escape with his life while his comrade had ridden off like the wind. He could say that, sadly, he thought his outrider had been captured, or worse, killed." I paused.

"Go on, Crach!" enthused the Abbot.

"But how do we persuade them?" Tudur threw in a valid question, the answer to which I was already about to give.

"We reward them with the assurance of safety, protection and money." I scratched at my beard. "We can only try and we might get even more insight into any other long-term plans Henry might have. My guess is he has none, except to delegate others to clean up the mess he creates. So, we would spawn the illusion, at least for the time being, their information is safe and Henry will probably reward them as well, so they cannot lose."

"Unless they screw up!" suggested Tudur.

"Well, we can but enquire of their willingness to comply and then decide from there." Owain was in agreement.

"Good," Tudur said getting back to his feet. "Let us go to the paddock and see how they fair now they have eaten. Perhaps their moods will be in our favour."

The paddock was but a stone's throw away and as we entered, both of the English soldiers were stood, ready to ride, and looking none the worse for their ordeal.

"Gentlemen!" Owain addressed them in perfect English. "I have a proposition to put to you."

Both soldiers stood quietly, listening intently with a self-knowing that the words they were about to hear may, indeed, save their lives. Emrys and Moelwyn stood nearby, hands on the hilts of their swords just in case anything were to go wrong.

"Are you loyal to your King?" Owain questioned them both.

The soldier who had worn the despatch satchel was short in stature but with strong legs and back from much riding. His weather-beaten face shone bronze. Under a sharp falcon-like nose, a large moustache drooped over his mouth to a pointed chin. He had sharp dark eyes, seemingly cheeky in their glance. He answered, "I am Jonas of Welshpool and am an Englishman. I am loyal to no English King but eat, I must, and I also have a wife and six children to provide for."

Owain smiled, sensing an opportunity.

"And you, Sir?" Owain turned to the other soldier.

"I am a soldier, Sir! I am loyal to whoever pays my wages. I have no family but I still have to eat," he answered. He was a big man, so plentiful food must be a priority for him.

"You do, indeed, my man. You do indeed!" Tudur slapped

him on the back enthusiastically.

"Well then, my proposition may fall as welcome words on your ears," Owain suggested.

"Indeed, it may," the Abbot smiled in recognition off the opportunity presenting itself, as did I. This was most fortuitous in the scheme of things.

"One of you will continue to ride to London with your dispatches, except you will go alone this time. When you reach the King, you will deliver the letters, together with a story of ambush which you managed to escape, not just with your life, but with the messages you now safely deliver. You will tell him that you fear your outrider has been slaughtered." Owain then asked, "Which one of you would be prepared to do that?"

The big soldier stood and, without any hesitation, said, "I am a soldier and I will fight for your army if you will have me." He sighed in resignation. "I have no desire to serve the English King."

"Then, you will join us!" Tudur exclaimed, slapping him on the back again. "We could use a bear of a man such as yourself!"

I was within earshot of Emrys and Moelwyn when I heard one say to the other. "Let's hope he doesn't betray us if offered more from elsewhere then. Eh?" The comment, whispered though it was, was clearly audible to me and thus must have also been heard by the Englishmen. But, fortunately, Emrys had spoken in Welsh, whereas the returned 'grunt' was a grunt in any language.

"And you, sir?" Owain asked Jonas.

"I will ride to London and relay your story," he replied.

The Abbot could hardly contain his excitement. "Good man! Good man!"

"Well, gentlemen, we have a bargain?" Owain looked for clarification.

"We do, Sir. We do," replied Jonas. "Would you like me to leave now?"

"Go when you wish, just stick to our story and hopefully the King will reward you as well."

We all laughed.

'Bear', as we had christened him, was busy with Emrys under the close eye of Griff.

Jonas began his journey to London at just before noon.

The plan, like a dragon's egg, was hatched.

CHAPTER NINETEEN

Carron the Raven pecked here and there and hooked a big juicy earthworm from the grass with his beak, tipping his head back, he quickly swallowed it in one gulp.

Sitting by the Pillar of Eliseg, I was contemplating the messages Carron brought from his brother ravens. He told me that Erasmus was very ill and his health was failing fast. Henry had ordered him to be moved to more comfortable quarters within The Tower and be provided with a fire and good food. But, as the saying goes, it was 'too little, too late'. It was thought that Erasmus was still likely to die quite soon. The news had been carried to the Council of Blue Stone and I wondered how they would view it.

In my mind, I felt it was only a matter of time before Erasmus faded away. The old man had been through too much but at least Henry had shown some mercy, although still demonstrated a distinct lack of any sense of loyalty to the old wizard who had served him so well. It was not only sadness that filled my heart, but it was also a sense of wrongdoing. There was so much cruelty between men in this world and poor Erasmus deserved none of it.

It was only a matter of time before the ravens left London to join their brothers in Wales. Henry had sealed his own fate by severing his links with the magical world through his actions against the old wizard. It would take a miracle to happen for the King if there were to be any change now. The die had been cast!

It was not only sorrow I felt for Erasmus, but also great sadness for the magical realms. This event would have wide-ranging consequences, the nature of which were presently hidden by the mists of the future.

Carron disturbed my thoughts with a splishing and splashing while taking a bath in the stream. He was a comical old bird and his antics always raised a giggle and a smile in me. Wolf lay under a nearby tree, his enormous head comfortably balanced on big paws as he snoozed. Cwtch was tethered to a dead tree on the other side of me, a gnarled stump surrounded by sweet short grass on which she quietly nibbled.

Perhaps I should eat. I was hungry and although the sun was with us today, it was still cold and damp. Gathering as many dry sticks as I could find, I built a fire for warmth and to cook. Warm drinks and hot food are just what I need at the moment. It might cheer me up a little too. My spirits were low and I should try to increase my energy as there was much to do.

I dozed with my back against the tree, feet warm by the fire, with a tummy full of valerian tea, fried duck eggs and bread. I felt more comfortable and a little less melancholy. Perhaps I could better describe my feelings as now being resigned to the situation with Erasmus. All was in the hands of the Gods.

It was getting chilly as clouds rolled over the sun and the sky darkened. Within no time, a few spots of rain dropped from the heavens. I gathered up my cooking pot, herbs and spoon, putting everything away in the saddlebag carried by Cwtch.

Wolf awoke fully, stood, gave a shivery shake of his entire self, licked his chops and strolled over to me. His tongue washed my face as he looked at me with affection. I stroked his beautiful head and ruffled his ears. The great wolf stared at me with hypnotic eyes and began to lick me again.

"Okay, Wolf, thank you. I love you too!" I told him as I gently redirected his nose from my face. Patting his head, I asked, "Shall we go and brave the weather?"

Wolf yipped as I climbed up my little rope ladder and settled comfortably into the saddle. Because I have such short legs and Cwtch's back is broad, I had put a sheepskin over the saddle for added comfort. It eased any discomfort on my bottom and certainly prevented the chaffing of my thighs which could be very painful.

Cwtch was a quite different type of horse altogether, compared to my old pony, Merlina. She was, of course, a much younger steed, with the fiery spirit to go with it. Riding her brought a new lease of life to me. I had become so accustomed to Merlina and we had both slowed down and aged together until I put her out to grass when she became too old for the long journeys I had to make. She was certainly not up to the hard riding required since the rebellion began. Merlina now grazed peacefully in the paddock at Sycharth, her days blissful and her nights warm and dry in a stable.

My relationship with Cwtch had come a long way since our first encounter at the portal. No longer was she frightened and skittish, but calm while still being spirited. She possessed a turn of speed which was quite remarkable for a warhorse. She reminded me of a magical mount, born to be ridden by dwarfs away from the world of man. The kind of horse legends are made of, the kind of horse spoken about in tales around the fire at the time between times.

We rode down the valley, with me, comfortable in the saddle, and Wolf gambolling ahead. Drops of rain began to fall, soon turning into a driving, beating downpour, blinding my view across the valley. Mist began to roll in and we needed to find shelter. With our heads bent into the wind, we rode on for an hour or so searching for cover. The rain did not let up and such was the ferocity of the downpour, it brought swelling streams and rivers to boiling white water, flowing swiftly on their downward path. With the ground still damp from recent rain, it quickly became awash with mud and even Cwtch found it difficult not to slip in the slime under her hooves.

The relief I felt when I spotted a familiar cave opening was immense. I soon had a fire roaring which warmed an inner cavern. Draping my clothes close to the flames, they soon began to steam as they dried out. I had rubbed Cwtch down as best I could and she stood dozing calmly in a corner, with one leg crooked and resting. I knew there was corn somewhere which I stored on a previous visit for Merlina, so Cwtch would not go hungry. Wolf had disappeared out into the storm and I suspected he would be hunting rabbits.

I put my pans onto the fire and seasoned one with some herbs and turnip. It would keep me going and warm my small tummy, there was no doubt about that. I was sitting in front of the fire, stirring my turnip stew, when Wolf came bounding around the corner into the cave, soaked through, and in his great jowl were two freshly killed rabbits. Whilst I skinned one for the pot, Wolf ate the other with very few bites, gulps and swallows. The fur and every piece gone with not a hair of evidence remaining. I speared mine from ass to mouth and placed it on the spit over the fire. It sizzled and spluttered as the heat reached the rabbit flesh and fat dropped on to the flames. It did smell good!

Wolf was laid by the fire, busy licking himself clean, steaming as his thick coat began to dry in front of the blaze. He kept gazing over at me and then averting his eyes to the rabbit, then back to me. I suppose he was expectant I would share my repast but then, of course, I would. He had, once again, provided a good meal. There was sufficient for me to have a good feed, share some with Wolf and still have some left over for breakfast. Wolf was welcome to a bit more than bones and scraps! He was a huge beast and one rabbit probably did not even touch the sides of his stomach. He glanced at the rabbit again and, after having completed cleaning himself, he laid down with his head across huge paws, eyes still shooting from me to the rabbit until he became drowsy, great eyelids starting to flicker, heavy with sleep, which was not far away. And still, the rabbit sizzled.

Dusk drifted in with yet more heavy rain and the storm intensified with thunder clapping in the distance, quickly followed by flashes of lightning streaking across a dark sky. I wandered to the outer cavern to watch from the dryness of the shelter. The rain still fell in torrents. Smelling the sizzling rabbit, I returned to the warmth of the fire and settled down to eat the wonderful roast that Wolf had kindly provided. It was not long before I was full of rabbit, washed down with turnip soup and herb tea.

Cwtch had her nosebag, Wolf had fallen fast asleep and was twitching in his dreams and I decided it was time to retire to my cot. Soon slumbering, I drifted off to sleep in the warmth of the cave, huddled under my sheepskins. The rain continued to fall, echoing in my dreams.

I woke some hours later and noticed the fire had died down to just a few glowing embers. I added some kindling and it quickly leapt back into life. I could still hear the rain falling outside, splashing onto the outer rocks. I loaded the fire with more wood to keep the inner atmosphere dry. It was still dark, so I climbed back under my sheepskins and soon returned to sleep. The next time I woke, light glinted in through a tunnel from the outer cavern. Dawn had arrived and with it, yet more rain. Flicking the sheepskin off my very warm body, I stepped down from the cot and added more fuel to the fire. Cwtch stood in the corner, still dozing, but Wolf was nowhere to be seen. I suspected he was out hunting.

My clothes were nice and dry, so I folded them up ready to put in the saddlebag. The cave was lovely and warm and I gave thanks for this sanctuary, as the rain continued to fall. It rained for most of the day and I was grateful to Wolf who had returned earlier with more rabbit for me to cook.

It was late in the evening before the rain eventually stopped and the moon began to rise in the sky. I saw little point in leaving now, so decided to spend another night in the cave. After a hearty bowl of rabbit stew, I soon fell sound asleep. This night my sleep would be invaded by dreams yet to come.

A mist, white, thick and seemingly impenetrable, surrounded me. I could hear voices in the distance and felt driven to walk towards them. At first, I heard only whispers, but the more steps I took, the voices faded as if they were moving away from me, or perhaps I was walking away from them. I became lost and disorientated, a fearful situation to be in for this dwarf who always liked to see clearly. The voices continued to come and go, from a whisper to being barely audible. I seemed to be walking around in circles and had no idea of how far I had gone or where I was walking towards, or away from either for that matter. This mist was too thick to gain any sense of direction. I could be walking into a trap. Suddenly, I experienced a surge in my dream body, as if something, or someone, had just taken hold of me by the ankle. The grip was strong, making it impossible for me to be able to walk at all and yet I saw nothing at my ankle. I felt chained, bound and disabled, while still being surrounded by thick white mist. Fear and a feeling of trepidation overcame me, an unwelcome sensation to anyone, but particularly to me as it makes me feel 'upside down', which is not a good sensation for this dwarf.

Time seemed to go on and on, yet nothing changed and the longer it continued, the more confused I became.

The mist began to lift and I could see a rainbow starting to emerge, bright, beautiful and extremely bold in colour. I saw a figure begin to appear and it was somebody I had no problem in recognising, it was Llwyd ap Crachan Llwyd, hovering in the most mystical of ways, which I was now so familiar with.

"Master, it is good to see you again," I greeted him.

"As it is to see you, Crach, but I come in haste in order to discuss your dream." Llwyd ap Crachan Llwyd shimmered in spirit form.

"This dream I am in, right now?" I asked.

"Indeed!" My old master and wizard appeared to sit down but I could see no seat beneath him.

"*The mist was thick, Crach and nothing could be discerned correctly, could it? Voices, distorted, direction unclear and never-ending?*"

"*Yes, this is true!*" I still could see no seat, and it was not for the want of looking.

"*This is, as you have probably already considered, a dream full of symbolism.*" A spectre-like hand twiddled with a ghostly wispy beard. "*What does it mean to you, Crach?*"

I was quiet for a moment or two, considering the symbolism of the dream, even though I was still in the middle of it.

"*Well, my first encounter of the mist was it being thick, impenetrable and never-ending. I was in the centre of it and felt isolated from much and especially that which I could not see.*" I paused.

"*Does that bare any significance to the issues that surround you at this time?*" Llwyd ap Crachan Llwyd took full advantage of my pause, interjecting and suggesting the symbolism of my dream enjoyed more bearing and focus in reality, perhaps not yet fully understood. "*And distant voices heard, coming and going with no discernible words and thus absent of meaning?*" he added quizzically.

I recalled the dream in its entirety, up to this point, just as my old Master directed. "*And so, I must prepare for the mist to clear.*" I now knew what he implied and the meanings became logical to me.

"*Indeed, you are correct, my fine Dwarf! When the mist clears, all that was previously hidden will be seen, that previously unknown will be known.*" Llwyd ap Crachan Llwyd emphasized his words.

I understood, nodding in agreement.

"*Clarity of the unknown will become clear, Crach, just as mountains do when the mist lifts.*"

His shimmering form started to fade and I thought I heard the call of a hawk.'

As my eyes opened, I awoke from the dream feeling alert and ready for the day. Sitting up on the cot, I could see sunshine blazing through the shadows in the cave.

There was not a hint of rain and the mist was gone.

CHAPTER TWENTY

Spring was in the air, with nights growing a little warmer and the days a little longer. All the rain gave essential water to the land and everything was beginning to sprout into new life. Grass, trees, bushes and wildflowers blossomed, nature was waking up after a long cold and hard winter. Rabbits emerged from burrows and dined on the sweet grass and birds of many shapes and sizes gathered twigs and bracken for nesting.

Merlina was in the paddock at Sycharth with Cwtch and other horses providing company for her, all grazing contentedly within the safety of Glyndwr's home.

Whilst I had been off travelling for the last two months, using the time to attend to my own matters, all else had been relatively quiet as the winter prevented any military action between the English and Welsh rebels. We, Welsh, were able to manage the harsh conditions in our mountainous land, we were used to it, but the English were not. Most of the army under Henry's command returned to London for the winter but a number had joined Hotspur to assist in reinforcing the English garrisons around North Wales. There had been no encounters worth mentioning as many of the English returned home to their hearths, huddling by fires whilst winter raged across the country.

Owain sat at a desk, a quill between strong and nimble fingers moved across the parchment, dipping for ink, scripting a letter to Hotspur. He paused for a moment and looked up at the rafters, seeking inspiration or divine intervention. Having gathered thoughts and intention, the quill met parchment once more as he continued to write.

I sat by the fire, reading an ancient book of spells and magic. I would like to say I was doing this purely from interest, but sadly it was of necessity. I knew the future was going to depend on my Prince, but he depended on me and I was going to need to use my skills in ways I had never been called upon to do before.

It was peaceful in Owain's private room and was reserved solely for his own use, apart from invited guests. I had sat in this room so many times over the last eighteen years and in this very chair. I no longer possessed a home to call my own. In fact, I do not think I ever really had one. So, I am content with my quarters here at Sycharth and it is where I keep my precious books, together with a few personal belongings, but I am a dwarf of few possessions. Clutter is such a thing in a man's life, but not for this dwarf. I suppose I could be described as a nomadic dwarf. I had my secret caves but nowhere was I more welcome than in my Prince's home.

Owain looked up from his work, quill still between his fingers. "Crach, we have had news from Lord Percy!"

"Ah, Hotspur?" I responded.

"Indeed, and our suspicions are correct. It seems that Henry has been duped by the messages we intercepted and..." he paused. "An announcement has been made. He offers rewards for my capture as well as the capture of my officers, but all others involved in the rebellion are offered an amnesty if they give us up, lay down their arms and return to their homes." He put down the quill and stared across the table at me. "He invites betrayal and mutiny, Crach!"

I stared into the flames and remembered the 'mist'. "Hotspur is as much of a tyrant as his master!" I remarked.

"That he may be, but this 'amnesty'? Do you think our men will betray us?"

"No, I do not, my Lord," I answered as I closed the book laying on my knees. "The rebellion is strong and the English words have yet to come to anything. We have experienced years of broken promises and austerity across our lands and this has taught us and proved beyond doubt, their words mean not a thing. So, I would suggest, my Lord, the amnesty would be as fruitless as the parchment it was written on, never to be used for any other purpose than our people to use to light their fires!"

"I am sure you are right, Crach. I just cannot help but have a small amount of doubt. Everything moved so fast until the winter came and now he invites surrender and mutiny!" Owain played with the quill feather, stroking his fingers along its edge.

"My Lord," I reassured him. "There will be no surrender. This is written in 'The Prophecy'."

"Then I will take your counsel, Crach, and concern myself

with what I was about before my mind was overtaken with doubt. I will continue to write to Hotspur," he said as he picked up his quill.

"What a splendid decision, My Lord, I will return to my book whilst you complete your writings."

The door opened and a maid brought in more wood for the fire. She laid it neatly against the wall and curtsied before leaving the room.

I returned to my book as Owain, head down, continued with his response to Hotspur. The only sound penetrating the silence was that of the quill scratching its way across the parchment.

"Right, that is that!" Owain said as he sat back in his chair and put the quill down. "It is done!"

"So, will you read it to me?" I enquired.

"Yes, Crach, I will. Your opinion would be most welcome." He stared at the parchment and cleared his throat. *"To Lord Henry Percy—dated the Nineteenth day of March in the year 1401.*

Sir,

Your notice to grant amnesty to the Welsh who are taking part in the rebellion is noted and frowned upon. You invite rebellion within a rebellion, turning Welshmen against their fellows with intention to cheat, lie and betray oaths of allegiance to the Welsh Crown.

I am Owain Glyndwr, Prince of Wales, and refuse all offers of amnesty on behalf of my people.

I invite you to stand on the field of battle with honour in the name of your King. Take heed, this Prince and his people will never surrender ourselves, our property or our land, to the English Crown.

Owain Glyndwr, Prince of Wales."

He took a little water to refresh a dry mouth and asked for my opinion. "What do you think, Crach?"

"I think that my Lord's words strike at the heart of the matter in hand," I replied. "You leave no room for negotiation as none would be appropriate and you invite him to meet you on the battlefield with honour, rejecting their offers for the falsehoods they are. The response is a good one, my Lord."

"Then we will send it to Hotspur!" Owain said, folding the letter and, using a candle, melted red wax onto the paper, stamping his seal as The Prince of Wales. A rider was summoned and the letter was on its way. Hotspur would receive it by the next day.

News of the amnesty spread across the North but none came forward to take personal advantage of the English offer. Nobody would betray their Prince as they had waited long enough for him to rise to the Crown. Now was never the time for surrender, in fact, just the opposite as winter gave way to spring, full advantage should be taken of every opportunity to strike against the English.

Chapter Twenty-One

Erasmus lay on a cot, his pallor grey against the pillow. The old wizard's breathing was laboured and very shallow, his chest hardly moving at all. His old heart was tired and his pulse weak and thready. Henry asked for the Court physicians to attend to the wizard's needs but, in reality, it was too late and there was little they, or anyone, could do. Erasmus was dying, of that, there was little doubt. He gasped and tired eyes opened briefly, taking in the scene of this, the final minutes of his long life—a life painted with wisdom, loyalty, magic and hard work. Here lay a man in the last throes of breath. He really did not deserve this lonely end. Henry may not have cut his throat or sent him to the block, but he had killed him by selfish intent and base cruelty. This was the way of the King, as many of his subjects were rapidly becoming familiar with it.

A physician wiped the forehead of the old man with a damp cloth, staring into his now open eyes. Erasmus stared back and began to mutter something, his lips moving but only inaudible whispers escaped. The physician had known Erasmus for over twenty years and been a friend to my old teacher, Master Healan, the apothecary. The physician, Master Smethurst, was no spring chicken himself and reflected on this fact as he looked into the face of his old friend with great pity and sadness. The old wizard's lips quivered again as he tried to speak. Smethurst bent his back and leaned an ear towards Erasmus' mouth, hoping he may hear whatever he was attempting to say. His voice croaked from a parched throat and his lips moved again, but this time, Master Smethurst heard the words.

"I am almost done with this life," he said, his eyes flickering with light and life still in them. "You must leave the City," he appealed to Master Smethurst. "As I pass to the spirit world, the magic within this kingdom will pass with me and the ravens will depart. It is written. The end of the King's reign will take many innocent lives with it." He coughed and began to choke. The physician tried to ease his discomfort but to no avail. Erasmus wheezed and coughed again. "Go, old friend. Go before it is too late!" Coughing, the old wizard convulsed from head to toe, gasping as the light left his eyes.

Erasmus was dead.

***

"So, the wizard is dead!" Henry looked out of the window with his back to Master Smethurst, who came to deliver the news.

"Did he have any last words for the world?" Henry asked.

Master Smethurst faltered in his reply before answering the King. He considered it was best not to share the final words of the late Court Wizard.

Smethurst was greying considerably at the temples as well as balding, which exposed a large wart on the top of his head. Deep-set eyes, bright blue in colour, peered from under very bushy eyebrows, giving the appearance of two furry caterpillars sleeping on his forehead. A wispy beard barely covered his chin but he had the longest neck imaginable, increasing his already great height.

"He died without uttering a word, my King," Smethurst lied. "He just went to sleep for the final time." A tear formed in the corner of the physician's eye, unseen by the King.

"So!" Henry began as he poured wine, raising a goblet to the heavens and made a toast. "May God grant you peace in death, Erasmus?" He drank deeply, then slammed his goblet onto the table.

"You may go!" Henry gestured towards Master Smethurst with a dismissive wave of the hand, clicking his fingers nonchalantly.

Master Smethurst bowed as low as his aged back would allow and walked backwards from the King's presence. Upon reaching the door, he stood up as straight as possible with such a lanky bent frame, turned to open the door and left the room.

Henry refilled his goblet and walked towards the window. Staring out, he noticed spring was upon the land. He marvelled at the gardens, not giving a second thought to the death of Erasmus, being just one more irritant in his life that would bother him no more. He drank deeply and over the rim of his goblet, he caught sight of six ravens taking flight from the royal gardens. They flew high into the sky as far away from

147

the City as their wings could take them. Henry was totally ignorant of the gravity of that which he had just witnessed.

The ravens, as predicted, were gone and would never return.

Chapter Twenty-Two

T an-y-Mynedd yawned, he was extremely tired and his responsibilities with the baby dragons were taking a significant toll upon him. His temper was a little shredded, to say the least!

"We have two more young dragons missing, Crach! I sent them down into the lower caverns to look for their brothers but I have no idea where they have gone to now!" He glared at the cave roof. "Certainly not up in the higher chambers, we have looked, so perhaps they are in the deeper caverns."

"When did they go?" I asked.

"Three days ago. Crow is beside himself and I do not need to tell you how guilty he feels, but it is not his fault, nor anybody's for that matter."

"And you have heard nothing since?" I sought clarification.

"No, nothing," he answered. "I would have gone myself, but I am just too big to get through some of the lower tunnels so I asked two of the youngsters to go instead."

"Three days is a long time, Tan-y-Mynedd." I was as concerned as he was now.

"It is. I am anxious for news and now we have five dragons missing." He rolled his eyes. "It will not do, Crach. It just will not do!"

"There are many to care for, my friend," I said, hoping to offer reassurance. "Things are sure to go wrong at times. Remember, it is not that long ago we thought they may all die, but for the healing skills of Faerydae."

"Yes, I realise this, Crach, but they are much bigger now and can get into a lot of trouble, and the sort of trouble we have not even thought of!" Tan-y-Mynedd sighed.

Crow stepped into the cavern, looking very depressed indeed. My old friend shuffled towards us with his head hung low on stooped shoulders.

"Crow, old friend!" I greeted him warmly, but his depression was too intense for him to respond. Tears rolled down his cheeks, dripping from chin to waistcoat, which was most sodden indeed from previous crying.

"Calm yourself, Crow." I put my arm around him. "Things are bound to go wrong at times—dragons will be dragons. You are a dwarf and this is not your fault."

"I know, but I can't help feeling so guilty." He snuffled into his handkerchief. "Fwynedd left to search for them but he has not returned yet either."

"He will," I told Crow, reassuringly. "How long has the shepherd been gone?" I asked.

"Almost a day," Tan-y-Mynedd confirmed.

"So, we have five missing dragons and one missing

shepherd?" My words were interrupted by Faerydae.

"We have," she said, passing Crow a dry handkerchief. "Fwynedd will return, I have a good feeling about that."

"And, the dragons?" I asked.

"I cannot see," she replied. "Something solid is preventing me from seeing with my mind. I do not know what, but I do know I cannot see through whatever it is."

"Ah!" Tan-y-Mynedd exclaimed. "The shepherd returns."

I turned to see Fwynedd the Shepherd stepping into the cavern. He was covered in dust, his hands and face thick with grime and mud.

"Fwynedd!" I welcomed him, but the familiar smile was absent from his face.

"You have grave news, Shepherd?" Tan-y-Mynedd suspected all was far from well.

"There has been a massive rockfall in one of the lower tunnels. So much rock has fallen from the ceiling, the tunnel is completely blocked and there is no way through. I tried an alternative route but was met with the same obstacle." He looked down at the ground in resignation. "If they are not yet dead, they are trapped and will starve to death."

"Is there no other way through?" I asked.

"No, not as far as I can see." Fwynedd rubbed his hands together anxiously. "I fear the worst."

"As do I." The great dragon looked very sad. "This is a tragic state of affairs," he added. "Five of our youngsters gone—five!"

"We cannot control nature," I suggested. "The rockfall was an act of nature."

"Perhaps nature conspires to rid the world of our species." He was serious and looked forlorn at such a prospect.

"I do not think so, old friend." But I knew, even though

he believed me, there was still a lingering doubt in his worried mind.

"We will see," he replied. "We will see." His voice trailed off as he looked thoughtful, saddened by these tragic events.

"There seems to be no way through," Fwynedd reminded us of the hopelessness of the rockfall. "If they were caught in it, there is little chance they could survive and have probably been crushed under the weight of so much rock."

"Well, on the upside of this calamity, there are still twelve living young dragons here in the nursery!" I said with more cheer than I could possibly feel, given the state of affairs we all found ourselves in. There were now only half of the dragons left from the twenty-four eggs originally found. The loss of the five babies was of great sadness to us all. Nobody could have seen this coming—nobody. There had been nothing revealed in the runes, no indication of this travesty at all from any quarter. This was nature at work. However, any form of understanding did little to raise our collective spirits. The fact of the matter was that five dragons were missing, dead or alive, we knew not.

Fwynedd raised his arms as if appealing to the heavens. "There are still babies to feed, even though babies they are no longer! Come, Crow, dry your eyes, my friend, we have work to do."

Crow nodded his head in silent agreement and followed Fwynedd out of the cavern.

"This is a sad time, Crach," Faerydae said as she placed her hand on my arm.

"There is much sadness in this world today," I replied. "Firstly, Erasmus and now, the dragons."

"Yes, but there is some brightness in every dark corner. That, you know better than most, don't you, Crach?" She gently squeezed my arm.

"Of course, but it does not make it any easier when we mourn those gone before their time."

"How do we know?" she said.

"Know what?" I enquired.

"That they have gone before their time!" I felt another squeeze.

"I know what you mean, Faerydae. I suppose it really means, we are not finished with those gone in our lives, whilst they are done with us by the mere fact they are no longer here. But it is a sadness, of that there is no doubt."

"I understand," Faerydae smiled warmly. "We can do little at the moment and perhaps the young dragons may have survived."

"But you could see nothing through rock?" I reminded her of her earlier words.

"True," she smiled again. "But that does not mean anything, apart from the fact, I cannot see anything at the moment. Perhaps this will change. Only time will tell."

"I agree, but only wish the news was not so full of sadness." I meant every word, in that any loss of life to me was a great sadness, life is just too valuable.

As Faerydae and I talked, Tan-y-Mynedd had fallen asleep. An enormous scaled head rested on huge legs. He had one eye closed and the other eye open. You will remember, dragons always sleep like this.

"What will you do now, Crach?" she asked.

"I will return to Sycharth and see what news there is. The King's agent, Hotspur, has invited surrender and amnesty, providing Owain is given into the King's hands. With this, together with what is happening to Erasmus, not to mention the dragon situation, there is much to consider." I knew I should use the time portal for speed but time to think was more important to me right now. "I think I will ride back. Time to think, together with fresh air, will do me much good," I added.

"Yes, I am sure it will," she smiled. "I must go and help with the dragons. Although, it is actually Crow that needs looking after right now. The dragons are doing very well. I am sorry." She paused. "I did not mean to dismiss the missing dragons as irrelevant. Not for one blink of an eye would I even think such a thing!"

"I know that, and no apology is needed," I reassured her.

Suddenly, we heard raised voices, then shouting, as Crow ran into the chamber, huffing, puffing and all of a fluster.

"Crach, Faerydae, Tan-y-Mynedd!" he stuttered in his excitement, gasping for air. "One, one of the dragons has returned!"

CHAPTER TWENTY-THREE

It was Triduum and Constable John Massy led the garrison of Conwy Castle to the parish church. The sun shone and it was a beautiful day. John Massy whistled happily to himself as they marched up the hill towards the church. There had been no further problems from the Welsh rebels, the garrison had been fortified with new supplies and a curfew kept the Welsh out of the way. All was well in the life of John Massy.

Thomas Easton, a carpenter, walked across the drawbridge to the Castle with his apprentice who carried two large boxes of tools. Thomas was originally from Chester and came to Conwy after his family passed with the plague. He was in his early fifties with a life of hard work and tribulations behind him. Thomas was not the most jovial of characters. Balding and portly, with a ruddy complexion, his face was pot marked and weathered. Thomas had strong hands and he clenched them nervously as they walked. Beads of perspiration formed and dripped from his forehead, but this was not a sweat brought on by the warmth of the day, it was due to anxiety.

"Calm yourself, Thomas," his apprentice whispered, prodding the carpenter in his back, playfully. "Just do everything as told you and all will be well."

The apprentice was tall and strong, a man in his forties and spoke with a cultured Welsh accent. A hood over his head shielded his features and he wore the clothes of a labourer, but something did not seem quite right about his posture. He carried himself more like a soldier than a carpenter's apprentice. He walked close to Thomas, whistling meaninglessly and tunelessly.

When they reached the door in the gate to the castle, Thomas knocked with his fist three times and a hatch opened.

"Master Thomas, it's you!" the 'face' said. "Who is that with you?" he asked. "I don't recognise him at all. Take the hood off!" The apprentice complied, smiling while pulling the hood back onto his shoulders.

"I'm the new apprentice to Master Thomas, Sir," he informed.

"He is, indeed, my new apprentice," Thomas added for good measure, trying not to appear nervous. This carpenter was quaking in his boots.

"Well, I don't know him, Master Thomas. Am I to take your word and risk the Constable's wrath if all is not as you say it is?" the 'face' asked.

Beads of sweat dripped from his head as Thomas reassured him all was as he said it was. The latch was drawn and the door opened for Thomas and his apprentice to step over the threshold. 'The face' closed the door behind them but before he could force the latch closed, the apprentice jumped on him, hitting him with a blow from a powerful fist, a fist that had felled many a man in the past. The 'face' slumped to the ground, unconscious.

"Tie him up!" the apprentice ordered Thomas, who complied as instructed, his hands trembling as he tied the ropes tightly. The 'face' stirred, groaning so the apprentice hit him harder this time and bedtime came early for the 'face'.

Thomas looked around nervously, hoping no solders had seen anything, but only a few remained and were busy elsewhere in the Castle.

A morning sun glistened across the doorway as the apprentice pulled an open latch and swung back the door. He whistled twice, two sharp blasts with fingers to his lips, and on the opposite side of the bridge, forty Welsh rebels appeared from nowhere and ran towards the door as fast as their legs were able. Little noise they made, but great speed they did. They quickly spanned the thirty or so paces before disappearing into the Castle. The apprentice slammed the door behind them and secured the latch.

Gwilym ap Tudur was no apprentice and neither was his brother, Rhys ap Tudur, who led the Welsh rebels across the drawbridge.

Rhys ordered his men to find the few soldiers who were still in the Castle and bind them. Two of his men ran to the tower and pulled up the drawbridge. The Castle was theirs and not a drop of blood had been spilt. The Tudur brothers from Anglesey had carried out Owain's instructions to the letter. Supplies had recently been delivered, just as the despatch letters to the King had manipulated and he, in his ignorance, had complied with. Now the supplies, and Conwy Castle belonged to the rebellion.

The Welsh secured the Castle and took their places on the ramparts, waiting for the English to return from their Triddum worship.

It was mid-day before the English garrison, led by Constable John Massy, marched down the hill from the church towards the Castle.

"Something's up, Constable. Look!" the Sergeant at Arms pointed to the Castle in the distance. "The drawbridge is up!"

"What?" John Massy strained his eyes and, just as was said, he saw the drawbridge was indeed up.

"Men!" the Constable shouted, stopping in his tracks. Turning to face the garrison troops, he exclaimed with force, "We are under siege! Make haste to the Castle!"

The Sergeant at Arms issued commands and the entire garrison moved speedily down the hill towards the Castle.

With the moat between them and the Castle, the English garrison stopped and looked up at the ramparts. The sight in front of their eyes was unbelievable. The flag of the King no longer flew, it was replaced by The Red Dragon!

"Christ!" Massy exclaimed. "Glyndwr's men have taken the Castle!"

Rhys ap Tudur looked over the ramparts and stared down at the English. He shouted at the top of his voice, "Happy Triddum, Constable, both to yourself and to your King!"

The Welsh soldiers standing at the walls burst into laughter and started to jeer at the English.

The Constable despatched a rider with all haste to Henry Percy, it was vital he knew what had happened. All of the garrison were ordered to take up positions around the Castle. As far as John Massy was concerned, the Welsh may have got in but they were not going to get out.

Chapter Twenty-Four

The gardens of Sycharth were beautiful at this time of year and as Owain and I meandered through the orchard, he talked about the dragons. I was surprised at his reaction to Tan-y-Mynedd's desire not to go to war.

"I understand his point of view, Crach. If I were a dragon, I would probably feel exactly the same," Owain said as he kicked playfully at a mushroom growing in the turf. "But it takes no imagination at all to see the advantages of dragons at our army's back in battle. But merely a dream, Crach, merely a dream."

I needed to bring him up to date with the situation of the missing youngsters.

"I have news from the Ffestiniog, Owain. Tan-y-Mynedd sent two of the young dragons down into the lower caverns in search of their brothers but just one has returned. After recovering from the shock of his recent ordeal, he has told Tan-y-Mynedd what actually happened. What has transpired is they caught up with the others in one of the lower caverns where one of them found a tunnel which was a route hitherto unknown. Having a curious nature, he entered it to explore and that was when the rockfall occurred, resulting from an enormous rumble in the belly of the earth. He said he only escaped because he caught up with the one who was climbing up the new tunnel and following him at speed, he managed to avoid the carnage left behind them. Stone and rock had broken away from the roof and totally blocked the tunnel behind him. A mist of dusty earth filled the air, making it difficult to breathe. But he knew his brothers were trapped under the fallen stone and that they could not have survived the crushing force of that much rock. So, he carried on following his brother up through the tunnel and eventually found themselves at the surface, close to the main entrance. When they saw the light for the first time, they were both quite shocked and confused. But the curious dragon stepped outside the cave into full daylight, looked around and flew to a nearby rock from where he had a clear view down the valley. His brother called to him to come back into the security of the cave and the watchful eye of Tan-y-Mynedd, but his request was ignored. The adventurous dragon then took off from the rock and soon disappeared from view.

Having been unable to persuade his brother to return, he found his way back down to Tan-y-Mynedd by the usual route from the surface."

"So, you are saying one of the dragons is flying out there somewhere, free for all to see!" Owain exclaimed

He was, of course, quite right, so I simply replied, "I am,

my Lord."

Owain looked up at the sky. "Where could it be? If it is seen and Edmund hears of it, we may find ourselves in the midst of a thunderstorm with nowhere to take shelter."

"This is a grave situation and, like the rockfall, one we could never have envisaged in a week of full moons." I felt quite despondent, as well as fearful. Owain was correct, this could be a travesty in waiting.

We all had to give a hand in doing what we could to find the missing youngster. Owain and Tudur were the only others away from the lair who knew about it. They would keep their eyes to the sky for sightings and ears to the ground for gossip.

I felt I should get back to Ffestiniog as soon as I could so I decided to use the time portal.

On my arrival, I learned Tan-y-Mynedd had been searching the mountains and valleys, long and hard. He would wait until it was dark before leaving the deep caverns and ascending to the surface. On the first night, the moon was in decline and a cloudy sky gave him cover for the flight he must take yet again. He had to find the young dragon. The great reptile lifted his powerful scaled nose to the air and huge nostrils flared as he took in all scents hidden in the atmosphere. He could discern nothing familiar so he took off, his huge wings giving one enormous flap, tail flicking, neck outstretched, he soared into the night sky, continuing to scent as he flew. A dragon's nose is the most sensitive of all creatures in the known universe, of this you will surely learn.

He flew all the way around the mountain that towered above their lair and then glided down the valley, silently, like a ghost.

Tan-y-Mynedd had no fear of being seen as his 'green smoke' would protect him, sending any unwanted onlookers to sleep and upon waking, they would have no memory of having seen a dragon and also have a blinding headache as a bonus to their amnesia.

His nose twitched, but still, no familiar scent entered those huge nostrils. He flew all night, perplexed by his inability to pick up even the faintest of scents that he could follow. But, the reality was, he was unable to detect anything because there was nothing there and this was a source of worry. How was it possible for the young dragon to just disappear without a trace? This, indeed, implied dark tidings. He returned to the lair as the sun cracked over the horizon at dawn.

For seven nights Tan-y-Mynedd continued to search the dark skies, avoiding human sight, and for seven nights, despite having flown for miles and miles, had found nothing.

"Perhaps he has gone to ground and found another cave," Faerydae suggested in an attempt to reassure the great dragon.

"You would find him if he was there to be found. Faerydae is right, it is the only explanation." Fwynedd was busy skinning a dead sheep in preparation for the youngsters' next meal. "Logic says, if we have not seen him, then nobody else will have either."

Crow snuffled into his handkerchief, "Oh, I do hope so, I do hope so!" He blew his nose rather loudly.

"Well, if he's dead, or alive, there is no trace of him anywhere on the land, or in the forest, but there are so many caves in the mountains so he could be absolutely anywhere. He flies well now, as they all do." Tan-y-Mynedd sighed the greatest of sighs and settled down for a nap.

"They say, 'no news is good news'." I hoped that to be the case, but 'no news' left me with much uncertainty and anxiety.

All remained quiet and as the days passed, still there was

no news. The young dragons were growing rapidly and were able to eat less often nowadays which gave Fwynedd a much-needed break after so many months of hard toil, although the shepherd, being who he was, had chosen not to rest, instead, he left the caves in search of the missing youngster. He may not have a dragon's nose, but his eyes and senses were still keen for one of advancing years.

Now we had thirteen young, growing dragons who were all able to fly well. Some may say that 'thirteen' is an unlucky number, but I like to think this is mere superstition and believe that in magic, it is a powerful number. Time will tell as to which fable is correct.

CHAPTER TWENTY-FIVE

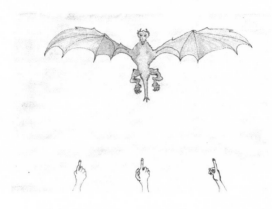

"We have seen their camp, my Lord. They have heavy horse and armour and hundreds of foot soldiers with pike and longbow. I counted an army of fifteen hundred strong," said Gogh.

"Fifteen hundred?" Tudur needed clarification.

"Yes, my Lord, fifteen hundred," Gogh confirmed his count. "There are Flemish amongst them and word says they have travelled from Pembroke in the south."

"That is one hell of a march, Brother!" Tudur remarked to Owain. "This is a formidable force. They will attempt to cut off any means of escape if we are attacked by Hotspur from the north."

"How many men do we have at arms now, Tudur?" Owain enquired.

"There are one hundred and fifty here in the compound and another three hundred more in the forest." He paused for a moment and then added, "We do have a lot of longbows and, of course, our sure-footed mountain ponies on our side."

"Good, as although we are outnumbered by more than three to one, their horses and army are heavy with armour. If we were on a battlefield of pastures, we would be slaughtered but we are in mountainous terrain so I suggest we withdraw even farther away up the mountain and wait for them. The mud, bogs, and rock will slow them considerably. If we make them chase us, I believe they will tire and when the rough ground holds them up, we will make our attack." Owain looked at Tudur and smiled. "We will win. Worry not."

The runes I cast earlier suggested a great confrontation but that guile and intellect would overcome the day and a great victory was predicted over adversity. It seemed to me as if the reading was referring to this imminent battle with the English. To have been able to create such a large force, Henry must have sailed his army around the coast and then marched them north, or, perhaps, he had gathered them from his garrisons in the south. It is possible that the Flemish mercenaries met them at Pembroke. The fact is, we could never know how, but all that really mattered was Henry's army was less than four days away so we had to move quickly.

Owain gave orders for his men to prepare to ride out at dark and meet up with our major force in the forest so that by the time the English appeared, we would be organised and in wait. After the evening meal, Tudur and a group of twenty-five rode out into the night. They were to mislead the English, taking them into our waiting trap. It was a good plan but only time would tell if it would work or not.

As the cock crowed, Owain and his men mounted their

horses and set off at a gallop to meet with the remainder of our force in the forest on the western slopes of Pumlumon, about twenty leagues from Aberystwyth. Tudur had orders to harass the English and lead them towards Owain's troop. This was a good place for a battle, their heavy horses and armour would quickly get bogged down and they would be unable to organise themselves. Our bowmen would take care of the rest and as Rhodri was in charge, hopefully, we would see a repeat of his last ambush where his men wiped out a force of English when they were also outnumbered by three to one.

Tudur and Will looked over the rock and down into the valley. The sun glinted and reflected from English armour and spear points as they marched along the path.

"They do not seem much organised," Will whispered to Tudur.

"Aye, they certainly seem to be lacking basic military skills, even their formation is naught but a disorganised rabble." Tudur scratched his chin. "Look at that!" He pointed at a small group of soldiers who had simply left the main contingent and squatted on the ground to start a fire.

A knight on an enormous white charger galloped towards them and seemed to be shouting, but they turned their backs on his protestations, carrying on with whatever they wanted to do. Fighting certainly seemed to be the furthest thing from their minds. The knight reined in his charger and galloped back to the main troop in frustration, leaving them in a cloud of dust and mud behind him.

"No discipline there, my Lord," observed Will.

"None, indeed, Will, which is bound to be in our favour." Tudur moved back from their vantage point into the scrub. He stood up and said, "Right, gentlemen! Let's have some fun!"

Tudur directed his small band of men efficiently. Despatching a few to take cover further up the pass, with their longbows at the ready. He sent two riders on fast horses to make themselves known to the front riders of the English army and told them to frustrate their path by leading them into a chase. The two set off at a gallop and on finding their vantage point, waited for the enemy to arrive.

The riders at point of the English force rode into the clearing, ignorant of what lay ahead of them. One whistled while daydreaming, whilst the other simply glanced here and there with no real interest in much, almost nodding off in the saddle.

As Tudur's men watched from the trees, they signalled to each other, dug spurs into their mounts and trotted into the clearing, just three hundred paces in front of the English riders. They both stood their mounts in a prominent place, where they would clearly be seen.

Suddenly, one of the English caught sight of the Welshmen, quickly taking him from his daydream, he shouted at the top of his voice, "Rebels! ...Welsh scum, after them!"

His co-rider came back to reality with a jolt and cried out "After them!" Reinforcing the alarm and call to chase. His horse reared and they set off after Tudur's men at the gallop. Hearing the cries of their fellows, more of the English retinue joined in the chase. Tudur's men simply turned their horses and rode like the wind, hotly pursued by the English but it was not long before their mounts grew weary, which was not surprising as they had already journeyed for days and covered many miles without much rest to reach North Wales. With English horses slowing and their rider's motivation waning, the two Welsh riders quickly shook off their pursuers.

Stopping on the ridge, both turned back to look for their

enemy and were surprised to see the small band that had been chasing them, had given up and turned their horses around to re-join the main force.

"This is going to be harder than we thought!" one said to the other.

"What a lazy rabble!" came the reply. "Give 'em a few breaths and we will try again." They dismounted and waited for the English to draw nearer.

"This game of 'cat and mouse' reminds me of my childhood," said one.

"Aye, 'you can't catch me'!" they both laughed and then waited in silence, watching the English as they drew closer. Fifteen hundred Englishmen, pursuing two Welshmen! Which was probably about right in the scheme of things to come.

"Now!" They both placed their mounts in full sight of the English, who responded with a little more zeal this time, pushing their horses hard in pursuit. The two Welsh riders gathered speed, twisting, turning and jumping over many rocks in their path, kicking up great sods of earth behind them, their destination, the site of the proposed battle site, drew close. They spurred their horses on and saw the slopes of Pumlumon ahead. Halfway up the hill, they split in direction with one riding to the left and the other to the right to avoid a bog which stretched across the hillside. The bog was deep in places, running the full pitch, and the English army was about to ride straight into the middle of it!

Nearly five hundred Welshmen lay in wait as the enemy rode onwards, oblivious to what was about to happen. Stakes, fashioned with sharp points, had been buried at an angle in a trench dug as deep as the height of a man. Fifty men stood behind the ditch with long pikes in their hands. Behind them, stood a hundred Welsh bowman with no shortage of arrows. Fifty bowmen lay in wait on each side of the hill, ready to catch the English in the crossfire. Hidden in the trees, over two hundred Welsh warriors sat in wait astride strong mountain ponies, who were well used to this harsh terrain. They were ready to ride down on the English, preventing any retreat they may attempt once the battle began.

As the English galloped up the muddy slopes of Pumlumon, they caught sight of the flags and banners in the distance. Upon seeing a line of Welsh soldiers, an order was given to 'charge' without so much as a pause for thought. Up the hill, they came—an enormous disorganised rabble with no real leadership.

Within a blink of an eye, over one hundred horses tripped and fell while trying to leap the ditch which suddenly appeared under their hooves. Riders fell onto the spikes, impaled, as their horses stumbled in all directions. More English rode into them and there was a chaotic mass of riders crashing into each other. When the second wave of riders became victims of the ditch, Owain gave the order to 'fire' and the bowmen let loose volley after volley of arrows, each one finding their mark as the English fell, one by one. Another volley of arrows and one hundred and fifty pike-men joined their ancestors. The English were in complete turmoil, riding into each other, horses trapped in the bog and as more came up the hill, arrows found them as they looked for cover which did not exist. Another hail of arrows and fifty knights fell from their horses as sharp points found the weak chinks in armour.

I sat astride Cwtch next to Owain mounted on his black charger, taking in the horror of what I saw, as he raised a banner from the ridge and Welsh riders appeared from trees on both sides of the hill, riding down hard on the English with broadswords flashing. Within no time, the remainder of Owain's small army fell on the English with a wrath many of the English or Flemish had never experienced before and most would never experience again.

English soldiers turned and tried to retreat down the hill but the Welsh horsemen cut them off, slashing swords until their foes were dead or badly wounded. They had no option but to surrender, discarding weapons onto muddy ground. The battle was over and those English who had managed to escape, ran down the slopes of Pumlumon—running for their lives. Owain's men captured those who surrendered. Two hundred of them sat wounded and bedraggled after the bloody battle, waiting Glyndwr's pleasure.

"Well, Brother." Owain thwacked Tudur's back. "We are victorious!" Both stood drenched in the enemy's blood, faces and hair stained and swords dripping.

"No sign of the King or Hotspur?" Tudur questioned.

"No," replied Owain. "But our paths will cross before long."

Owain's men cheered and cheered. They had defeated an English force three times larger than themselves and had certainly proved their worth on the battlefield today.

Owain and Tudur simultaneously looked up to the sky with others following their gaze, several of them pointing skywards.

"Dragon…a dragon!" came a shout from the battlefield.

Chapter Twenty-Six

"**B**y dragon's breath! Owain it is the young dragon!" I said.

"Be still, Crach. Wait." Owain gestured back to the sky where the dragon disappeared behind a cloud.

"They have all seen it, My Prince, even the English. There is no way we can hide this now."

"He has gone," Tudur whispered.

But it was, indeed far too late to keep this a secret. Both English and Welsh saw the dragon in the sky.

"I can order our men by Royal Command not to discuss what they have seen," Owain offered.

"I do not think it would help, my Lord," I replied. "In fact, it could make things worse. At the moment, only one dragon has been seen and perhaps, as far as everyone else is concerned, it is the only one there is. The reality facing us, my Lord, seems to be that we may have to sacrifice one in order to protect the rest."

"I see, Crach, a good point to make." Owain tried to look hopeful but he knew how serious this matter had just become.

"He has gone now, Crach, so nothing for them to see any more." Tudur patted me on the shoulder.

"But plenty for English and Welsh alike to gossip about and who knows how the story will grow, given how many eyes have witnessed the dragon." I felt very sad, and this was becoming a habit!

The implications of this reckless young dragon's behaviour could be catastrophic, but only time would tell and I hoped it would all be resolved soon and without too much difficulty. It was clear to me that the young dragon had been hiding somewhere but never should he be flying in daylight, this was strongly discouraged by all dragons and this was one very important lesson he should have paid attention to.

"What will you do now, Crach?" Owain enquired.

"I am of a mind to return to Ffestiniog in haste to talk with Tan-y-Mynedd." I was really beginning to feel quite upside down and, as you well know, I do not like this at all.

"Things are not quite going to plan, are they, Crach?" Tudur said, putting his sword back into the scabbard at his waist. "We could not have foreseen this!"

"No, we could not," I agreed. "But here we are, and, it is what it is."

"We must away to our hiding place, Crach, before Hotspur appears," Tudur said.

"He will not appear, Tudur," Owain said with preconceived confidence. "Remember we changed the information in their letters and even though this battle may have taken all by some surprise, Hotspur will not know of it for at least two days."

"So, we can now deal with the rewards of battle. It's time to loot the vanquished!" Tudur strode off to join others who were searching the fallen knights for trinkets, treasures and money.

"I will leave you to the spoils of battle, my Lord. I must return to Ffestiniog," I said.

"Of course, Crach. I will see you soon, no doubt," Owain waved as I rode Cwtch away from the battle site.

I would have half a day's ride to reach the time portal but perhaps we could make it sooner. I spurred Cwtch into a gallop.

CHAPTER TWENTY-SEVEN

R hys ap Tudur stood on the battlements, staring down at
the sight greeting him on the other side of the moat. As
the Welsh now held Conwy Castle, Rhys saw himself as the
new 'Constable' and, in front of him, the former Constable,
now 'Master' John Massy, sat in full battle armour on a black
charger with a retinue of bowmen and English soldiers behind
him. Behind them, sat on a large white stallion, was Henry
Percy Hotspur, looking a formidable sight as the sun reflected
from his armour.

John Massy came forward and hailed the rebels inside the
Castle. "We would have parley with you. Will you speak?"

Rhys appeared between the stone battlements and raised
his hand, then bows made of elm, strong and powerful,
charged with arrows, appeared in the hands of Welsh archers.

Their eye upon the target below—the English.

Hotspur was a seasoned soldier, and also no fool. He recognised he could lose many men in this situation. They sat at a distinct disadvantage with their own archers unable to get true arrows off, whilst the rebels would have no problem in slaughtering his men where they stood. The reality of the matter was clear in Hotspur's mind. When Henry heard of the siege, he ordered Hotspur to take back the Castle and kill every rebel, capturing and executing those not killed during the assault. He had his orders and knew a fight was at hand but had to try and talk the rebels into surrender in a futile attempt to save the lives of his men.

John Massy raised an arm to the several lines of bowmen, now poised and ready to let loose their arrows.

"Will you speak?" John Massy repeated.

Rhys moved forward with a broadsword in hand and stared down at Massy below. "What is it you want, Englishman? This is Wales, our country, and you have no right to be here anymore. If you value your lives, then gallop off into the ether." He slammed his broadsword down onto the stone, sparks splintering. Clearly, Hotspur's defence should be to withdraw from sight.

Hotspur dug his spurs into the great white stallion, urging him to walk on. He joined Massy in front of the castle and this time, he shouted up at the battlements. His voice was firm, cultured and very English. "Rhys ap Tudur, it is Henry Percy, I pray you hear my words."

"Oh, you do, do you?" Rhys questioned. He knew Hotspur, having previously fought in campaigns alongside him and he was one of the few Englishmen he respected.

"I do," Hotspur replied. "I know you Rhys ap Tudur, as you know me. I order you to vacate the Castle and surrender in the name of the King. You are all guilty of high treason and will be executed."

Rhys laughed raucously, as did others who could understand the English tongue.

"So, my Lord Percy. You expect us to lay down our arms, walk out of the Castle, hand it over to you, and then stand by and do nothing while you kill us all!" Rhys laughed again.

"The King has given me no choice in the matter, Rhys ap Tudur. As much as it may pain me, I have my orders and my duty!"

Lord Percy turned his horse and gestured to John Massy, with a flick of his head, to do likewise.

"And I have mine!" Rhys retaliated—"Fire!"

The bowmen loosed their arrows at the English on the other side of the moat. Their elm bows and arrows could kill a man at three hundred paces, so the English were well within range and the rebels were expert archers.

Arrows rained down while a few of the English bowmen managed to string an arrow in return before they fell to the ground. Lord Percy ordered a withdrawal so that his troops were sufficiently out of range of the Welsh arrows. Seeing the retreat, leaving dead and wounded scattered on the ground, the Welshmen ceased firing, not wanting to waste their arrows. They cheered like mad men, half-crazed in victory.

Lord Percy looked at the carnage in front of him. Over fifty of his men lay dead or seriously wounded. This was not going to be easy, but he ordered the siege ladders to be brought forward and his archers to load their bows.

Rhys watched and called to his brother, Gwilym ap Tudur, who was on the other side of the battlements. "They prepare to come again, Gwilym!"

Gwilym ordered the bowmen to ready themselves.

Lord Percy gave the command to fire and a hail of English arrows bounced off the Castle walls. Soldiers, carrying long siege ladders, used the cover of fire to advance towards the Castle. They had gone but a few paces when Welsh arrows returned with such ferocity that many English fell to the ground. Again, the English loosed a hail of arrows and again, they bounced off the stone walls of the castle. Siege ladders advanced towards the walls, but yet another torrential downpour of arrows fell on the English. Arrows met eyes, necks and heads, killing instantly. Others met arms, legs and torsos, wounding and disabling. Soldiers fell scattered on the ground around the drawbridge, bodies piling higher with each volley of arrows released.

A couple of ladders reached the Castle walls, but as soldiers attempted to prop one of them up, hot oil and sand prevented any insult to the Castle as it showered down on the English. The wooden ladders ignited to flame, English soldiers scorched and burned black by the oil fell from the walls. The other ladder successfully stood leaning against the wall, erect and stable as English infantry began to climb. As the first man reached the top, he was greeted by Gwylm's broadsword coming down hard on his head, splitting the skull in half. Two Welsh soldiers grabbed pikes and pushed the ladder away from the castle wall and twenty English soldiers fell, broken on the ground.

Lord Percy signalled a withdrawal and those who were able ran away from the Castle Walls as quickly as they could. Massy raised a white flag and requested the recovery of the dead and wounded. Rhys gave orders for bows to be dropped and the Welsh watched as the English carried their countrymen away from this place of battle.

Now Lord Percy must seek counsel from the King.

Chapter Twenty-Eight

The coach-house was very busy tonight and strumpets rushed here and there, serving the many men who had come to drink and celebrate the success of the rebellion. Pipe smoke, sweat and grime of men, mingled with smells of stale ale and food cooking in the kitchen. Such an establishment welcomed travellers and merchants alike, but it also enjoyed a healthy patronage from the locals thereabouts.

With the recent successes at Mynydd Hyddgen and rumours of the capture of Conwy Castle, those supporting the rebellion were in high spirits. But, at a time like this where rebellion raged over the land, lurking in the shadows lay the unknown, being no different in this establishment than in any other.

Three strangers sat in a corner hidden from the light,

dressed in once fine clothes, now dirty and stained from weeks of hard riding and searching, but searching for what? They drank their ale in a quiet manner whilst looking, listening and observing everybody in the bar. Their eyes scoured the room.

"Did you see it?" a small man with a scar running down one side of his face, from eyebrow to chin, shouted to friends.

"It was huge and flying high up in the sky!" his companions mumbled in agreement.

"Never seen anything like it," said one.

"Only ever heard of them in fairy stories," said another.

"Bloody big, it was!" came a voice from the other side of the room.

"Well, we all saw it," added another.

"Yes, but did we? How could we have? They do not exist!" said a big man with a hump on his back.

The ears of the men in the shadows pricked, this conversation could be of interest so they listened intently, bending heads towards the voices.

"So, if we saw it, and we all saw it, even the English, then it must have been real," somebody else suggested.

One of the shadows in the corner whispered to his friends, "What are they talking about?"

"Sounds most interesting." came the reply as the chatter in the bar continued.

"Well, it flew away anyway," the voice said.

"Don't matter really, because now we know they do exist. Has to be a good omen, I would say," the hunchback suggested.

"Yes, a great omen for the rebellion. Whether it was real or not, a dragon in the sky over Wales has to be a good sign," somebody else chirped up.

When the word 'dragon' emerged in the conversation, one of the three shadows sitting in the corner nearly fell off his chair in surprise. Another shadow dug his friend in the ribs and when their faces met, the look of surprise was equal to their master, who was now in the midst of regaining his composure.

"Where was this?" a voice hailed from the shadows.

"Over the battlefield," came the reply.

"Battlefield?" questioned the man in the corner.

"The battle of Mynydd Hyddgen, last week. We hammered the English into the mountain bogs!" The hunchback looked into the shadows for the source of the voice.

The men in the shadows knew nothing of a battle, having been on the road for months, hunting and searching for rumours and information about dragons. Now, here they were and, suddenly, without asking, they found some evidence rather difficult to refute as so many had witnessed the sighting. It had to be real. Edmund could not believe his luck after so many weeks searching on the King's orders for this mystical dragon and now, just as he had almost lost hope, success may be on the horizon.

His comrades began to gather their few possessions and digging Edmund quietly in the ribs, said, "Let's go."

Edmund picked up his sword and hat and quietly followed his men out of the coach-house, slipping away unnoticed.

Standing by the stables, the three men collected their horses and checking they were not being watched, quietly mounted.

"So, we are not on a fool's errand, My Lord," one remarked.

"It would appear not," Edmund said, hoping he may yet find favour with the King.

His appeal to return to Court had been snubbed and on a recent visit to Hotspur, he was given a letter from the King, essentially suggesting if he ever returned having failed in his mission, then he must be resigned to losing his head! To all intent and purpose, this made Edmund an outcast. Not in a month of Sundays was this something he had ever envisaged for himself. The conversation witnessed this evening could change his luck considerably.

"Let us ride to Pumlumon, where the battle took place. Perhaps we may find something there," suggested Edmund.

"Yes, my Lord," one of them answered. "This is getting exciting," he added.

"Indeed," said the other.

As they rode off into the night, a raven who was perched on the stable roof, listening to every word, flew off after them, keeping distance and silence.

The sun was on the rise as the three riders arrived at the site of the recent battle. A few bodies remained but most had been taken away, although dead horses lay everywhere, the carcasses having been ravaged by crows and wolves.

Recent rain made the ground even more treacherous. As they rode along, one of the horses stumbled, sending its rider headlong into a swampy bog. As he struggled to get out, he felt himself being sucked further down and the more he struggled to rid himself of this unearthly trap, the deeper he sunk in.

"Help me! In the name of God—help me!" he screamed to Edmund and his friend.

"Christ!" his friend exclaimed as he leapt from his horse while grabbing a rope to throw out to him. He slung it as far as he could but it was just out of his friend's reach, so he reeled it in and tried again. This time his friend was able to grab it with his left hand but as he lunged, the bog sucked him in further until only an arm with a hand holding the rope and head were visible to the others.

"Tie it around yourself, then I can pull you out!" shouted his friend.

The man in the bog struggled to do as advised but the bog was too thick, it restricted his every movement and with every flinch of a muscle, the slime continued to suck him down. His nose was now going under and bubbles of spent air appeared as the rope became taut. His friend desperately shouted at Edmund to come and assist when suddenly there was a loud devilish screech from the sky which drew their eyes. In total shock, the rope was dropped as they saw a dragon flying over the hill, landing rather clumsily not three hundred paces away! It was about the size of a large cow with a scaled body, wings and a tail. It dug its snout into the belly of a dead horse and began to feast, oblivious to anything apart from relieving its hunger.

In silent shock, Edmund and his companion watched with amazement as the dragon feasted on the deceased horse. Hearing bubbles rise to the surface of the bog, they turned to see their co-conspirator gone forever into the bowels of the earth. They both stood speechless and transfixed. Edmund, ignoring his drowned comrade, dropped to his knee and gestured silently for his companion to do likewise.

"How will we catch it?" Edmund whispered.

"I am not sure we could," came the reply as the ruffian, transfixed by his partner's recent demise, stared down into the bog.

"Hang on!" Edmund grew a little excited, while still managing to keep his voice at a whisper. "What if I used poppy juice to send the beast to sleep? We could pour drops of it onto a horse carcass."

"Now, that is a good idea, my Lord. It is bound to return here to feed whilst ever there is meat to fill his belly. We should hide under those trees for now, we do not want it to see us," he suggested, turning his mind from his friend's death to the task in hand.

The two crawled away towards cover as quietly as they could. On seeing the dragon raise its head from feeding, look around and sniff the air, both stopped abruptly, freezing every muscle and sinew of their bodies.

They breathed a sigh of relief when the beast returned to its meal. "That was close, my Lord."

Especially keen not to draw the attention of this huge reptile, Edmund agreed with a nod of his head and they stealthily continued to creep away to cover, away from the bog and the dragon's eyes. While they secreted themselves under the trees, Edmund dug deep in his saddlebag, searching for the bottle of poppy juice he had been given by Erasmus some time ago. His fingers found the small glass bottle.

"If we put this in a carcass and the beast eats it, sleep will come quickly, then we can chain it and deliver it to the King. Imagine the glory we will receive!" Edmund enthused quietly, attempting as much restraint as possible in his excitement.

"Well, my Lord, I think it may be a little more difficult than you describe. I mean, it ain't exactly a pussy cat, is it?" he sneered at Edmund. "Then we will need a wagon and cage so we can get it to London, unseen! Sorry, my Lord, I mean no disrespect, but you must be deranged."

Edmund glared at his companion, unable to explode into a full rage as he usually would for fear of scaring the dragon away or, worse still, attracting it to them. They continued to watch the dragon from the cover of undergrowth beneath the trees. Having eaten his fill, the reptile staggered clumsily up the hill, flapped large wings twice, extended its neck and left the ground, disappearing over the ridge.

"He'll be back," Edmund said. "Now I must drug a carcass and wait for him to become hungry again."

"It might be several days yet, my Lord," his companion said.

"Then we will wait several days!" asserted Edmund.

For a moment, he played with the bottle of poppy juice he was holding, playfully tossing it from one hand to the other.

"On second thoughts, I want you to go and get a wagon and an animal cage from the town in the valley," said, Edmund.

"A wagon won't be difficult to find, my Lord, but an animal cage large enough for that beast? I don't know how easy that will be!" He did seem genuinely concerned. He did not like Edmund at all, but now his friend was dead, he only had him for company. "I will do my best though," he conceded.

"Good," replied Edmund. "And I would like you to go now!"

A raven took flight from a nearby tree.

Chapter Twenty-Nine

The speed at which Cwtch galloped to the time portal meant it took less than half a day to reach. Tethering her safely to a tree, I entered the portal to Ffestiniog and was soon sitting with Tan-y-Mynedd in deep discussion regarding the missing dragon. Although missing, as such, no more, because he was seen flying over the battle site in broad daylight by both English and Welsh Soldiers at the end of the Battle of Mynydd Hyddgen!

"It was a fierce battle," I told Tan-y-Mynedd. "Many lost their lives, both English and a few Welsh. Horses fell by the hundred, old friend, it was carnage."

"So, he witnessed the battle and would have smelt the blood, Crach!" Tan-y-Mynedd commented. "He will probably go back to feed on the dead when his hunger strikes."

Faerydae entered the cavern with Carron on her shoulder. "We have a visitor, Crach!"

Tan-y-Mynedd swished a huge scaled tail. "Ah! The big blackbird comes to my lair."

Carron and Tan-y-Mynedd tolerated each other, after all, they were both very magical creatures and knew more than most about everything.

"I am a raven, as you well know, Lizard!" Carron had his turn.

Faerydae and I smiled at each other, amused by their wordplay.

"Why are you here?" I asked. "Has something happened?"

Carron told us that one of his brothers has been trailing Edmund and his cohorts. "He followed them to the battlefield at Pumlumon where one was sucked into the bog. He listened carefully to a plan they were hatching to drug the dragon with meat soaked in poppy juice, then cage him and take him to the King!" Carron squawked and fluttered his jet-black feathers.

Tan-y-Mynedd was furious at learning of such a plan, snorting anger, smoke billowing from his nostrils, fortunately, without ignition to flame. "This will not happen! It cannot happen! If Edmund succeeds in this plan, all will be in great jeopardy and especially the life of the youngster. No! I will stop this." Tan-y-Mynedd extended his neck and looked straight into my eyes. "This is a job for dragon and dwarf, Crach!"

I knew what he meant and agreed. Only he and I could carry out this difficult task so we prepared for the flight to Pumlumon, to what was now a graveyard at the site of the Battle of Mynydd Hyddgen. We would leave as soon as darkness fell.

"I will join you both," squawked Carron, alighting from the ground and flying to my shoulder. "To be able to succeed, we will need all the magic and guile the three of us together can muster. All ravens are now loyal to Crach and, by association, also to the dragons. Now, we are all brothers." Carron stared at the great dragon who, I swear to you, I saw smile in a way only a dragon can.

At least the remaining dragons appeared to be in good health under the caring hands of Faerydae, Fwynedd and Crow.

As night began to fall, dragon, raven and dwarf made their way to the surface through the tunnels of Ffestiniog. I climbed up the huge scaled leg of my old friend and made myself comfortable between his armoured shoulders, where I have sat many times before on numerous flying expeditions. Tan-y-Mynedd stretched his neck and stood erect, a pronged tail flicked and with one flap of his enormous wings, we soared up into the night sky, hotly pursued by Carron the Raven. We flew towards the moon, silently, unseen and with great purpose in mind. Tan-y-Mynedd glided down the valley under the cover of shadows, left and right, great wings tipped appropriately as he bade each sinew to his will.

He set down just behind Pumlumon on the ridge. Fortunately, the night was devoid of light with thick clouds concealing both the stars and the moon. Tan-y-Mynedd settled his huge wings and squatted down. I climbed from his back and slid down his side to the ground. Carron landed rather clumsily on my shoulder, but quickly righted his imbalance at my expense as talons gripped hard, clinging on tight!

We looked over the ridge, down the valley into the shadows to where the battle had taken place. Suddenly, clouds swept past the moon and light broke over the mountainside. We could see the carcasses of dead horses, nothing more. But suddenly, a horse neighed in the distance and, even though sound travels further at night while most else is sleeping, saving the creatures whose day is our night, it was almost certainly on this side of the valley and seemed to have come from under the trees, just beyond the carcasses.

"I will take a look to find where the neighing horse stands," Carron whispered as he silently took to the air, flying off in the direction of the horse's protestation.

This had been a fierce battle with many English perishing under arrow and sword of the rebellion. Our forces had not gone unscathed this time and we had suffered the loss of some of our warriors, with many wounded also. Owain's strategy had worked perfectly as Tudur and his men led the English into the trap. Once trapped, Glyndwr's cavalry, on sturdy Welsh Mountain Ponies, swooped down, cutting off any possible way of retreat the English could take, but sadly, of course, there were casualties. Now the bodies were gone and only ghosts of the dead remained to haunt the mountainside. Many Welsh and English saw the dragon after the battle ended and somewhere down there in the forest, lurked Edmund, and, somewhere else, was the dragon.

Carron returned a moment or two later. In silence and with great precision, he landed on a nearby branch. He is not well known for this type of landing! Tonight, though, it was essential we did not make a sound that may draw attention from unseen eyes.

"He is down there, amongst the trees," Carron relayed to us what he had seen. "There are two of them. One of whom I recognise as Edmund, the other, I suppose, is his surviving cohort. There are also two horses and a wagon under the trees. His cohort is sleeping on the wagon whilst Edmund is keeping an eye on a carcass laying not far from where they hide."

"We could sneak down and capture them, but that might prove difficult," I suggested. "How can we succeed in getting down there, but, then again, what would be the point?"

"There isn't one," said Tan-y-Mynedd quietly. "We might as well wait until the youngster arrives, as he will do, then we can deal with it all in one go. We still need to persuade him to return to the other dragons and that might not be easy now he has had a glimpse of the outside world and been successful in finding his own food."

I agreed with him so we settled down, taking it in turns to keep watch with our eyes peeled on the mountainside below the ridge where we sat in wait. The night was not a cold one but a fleeting chilly wind blew from the north. I pulled the collar of my sheepskin jacket up around my neck for extra warmth. Tan-y-Mynedd dozed with one eye open and Carron the Raven stood motionless—a big black bird, magical and serene, a silent silhouette on the ridge, keeping watch on all below.

It was a long night and mostly silent, with the exception of an occasional howl of a wolf, his call returned from many miles away by another. A dog fox barked and yapped, a rabbit screamed its last scream, probably being an early breakfast for the fox. There were also hoots of owls and the screech of a hawk. Although this might seem like hours filled with the sounds of the 'creatures of the night', the silence in between their calls was dark and eerie and under the circumstances, deafening.

Dawn was approaching and the darkness of the night began to lift with very few clouds in the early morning sky.

Over our heads, the stillness was interrupted by a flapping of wings. We looked up and saw the young dragon gliding down, landing in a rather ungainly way, close to the two carcasses near the trees. Gathering himself up, after landing with a thud, the young dragon sniffed the air and looked around. He had not seen us when he flew overhead and as we were upwind of him, he did not detect our scent.

"He has grown well," Tan-y-Mynedd observed.

"He is certainly surviving," I added.

"He is a dragon," Carron chirped in.

We watched as the young dragon sniffed at the carcasses, making his way towards them with an ungainly waddle. Bending his snout forward and tearing off a piece of horse meat with sharp razor-like teeth, he tipped his head back, outstretched his snout to the sky and swallowed. As the raw flesh disappeared, his throat moved rhythmically as if in the midst of dance. Dipping his head, the young dragon tore off more flesh, chomped and swallowed. A piece of meat fell to the ground as he chewed, and in a flash, his head swooped down, teeth gripped, jaws munched and throat gulped.

In the trees, hidden from view, Edmund and his assistant stood in silence as the dragon ate. Edmund had dosed both carcasses with poppy juice, ensuring that whichever one the dragon chose to eat, a drug-induced sleep would be the only result, whereupon they would put him in the cage, cover it and take the captured dragon to the King. Well, that was the plan anyway and it seemed simple enough.

As we looked on, Carron took to the wing in order to check what was going on with Edmund and his companion. I stared at the magnificent sight in front of me, forgetting for a moment the gravity of our situation. What an incredible specimen he was growing into. Similar to Tan-y-Mynedd in every way, except in size, being only a quarter grown. The young dragon looked proud. He was gaining strength but as yet had no experience of life and was certainly ignorant of the dangers lurking but a few moments away.

Tan-y-Mynedd stared at his charge with a certain amount of pride, but also with a certain degree of frustration, in that we were all in this predicament because of his youthful exuberance and he could be responsible for leading the other young dragons to their premature demise.

The young dragon continued to feast on the tainted carcass, mouthful after mouthful, shaking his head and swallowing every morsel. As we watched from our vantage point, Edmund looked on from his.

"He has a good appetite," Tan-y-Mynedd observed in a whisper.

The youngster stopped eating and sat back on his haunches with bits of half-chewed horseflesh falling from his jaws, which dropped gaping open, all control now disappearing. His eyes began to roll then, all of a sudden, with no warning at all, the young dragon crashed headfirst onto the ground, fast asleep. The effects of the poppy juice had worked well.

After the young dragon had fallen to the ground, Edmund and his co-conspirator slowly crept from their hiding place in the trees. Edmund stared at the sleeping dragon in wonder. "Did you ever see such a thing?" he remarked.

"Not in this life!" came the reply.

"He is sound asleep. Fetch the wagon!" Edmund ordered.

"So, now is our time, Crach. Climb on my back." Tan-y-Mynedd invited me, in a low calm voice.

I slowly and quietly did as I was bid with a certain degree of apprehension, I must say, being unaware, as we all were, as to what may happen next. Tan-y-Mynedd flapped his wings and we soared into the air. Edmund and his sidekick were far too busy to notice us as we glided above. They were attempting to lift the young dragon into the cage on the back of the wagon. This was not an easy feat as the youngster was not exactly a lightweight and Edmund lacked physical strength, so most of the labour fell on the soldier's shoulders.

As they struggled, Tan-y-Mynedd circled above waiting for his moment and then, without warning, swooped down. Within a blink of an eye, we landed right in front of Edmund. Their horses went crazy with fear as Tan-y-Mynedd roared. Edmund's horse broke free from its tether and galloped away as fast as it was able, with terror oozing from every pore. The horse between the shafts of the wagon panicked and reared, jolting and buffeting until the staves snapped and it too galloped off, following its companion.

The young dragon lay on the ground, oblivious to all going on around it, lost in the dreams of poppy juice.

Edmund stood rooted to the spot, paralysed with shock and trepidation. A damp stain appeared on his breeches, not surprisingly his bladder lost control when confronted by such a beast as Tan-y-Mynedd. Logically, who could be surprised at his reaction as he now faced a dragon four times larger than the one he thought he had captured. All thoughts of glory were now just a passing whim. Henry would never believe this story if, indeed, he survived to tell the tale.

Tan-y-Mynedd reared up again and spat fire into an empty space. Edmund wet his breeches for a second time, whilst his companion picked up a pike that was lying dormant on the battlefield and thrust it at the great dragon.

I felt it was a brave, yet foolhardy, gesture. As the pike struck Tan-y-Mynedd's armoured leg, his great snout turned and in the wink of an eye, he lunged at his attacker who tried to step aside, but to no avail.

The great dragon was now in a fierce temper. They had not only drugged his ward in an attempt to either kill or kidnap him but now they attacked him too. Tan-y-Mynedd was furious which resulted in him picking up the petrified man in his jowls. Screaming and struggling, the helpless Englishman screeched in agony as huge sharp teeth punctured his thigh. Blood gushed from a severed artery as the great dragon threw up his head and tossed the man into the air, then with a great fiery breath, Tan-y-Mynedd expelled hot air and flame, engulfing the man in mid-air, killing him before he hit the ground. The great dragon turned a huge head swiftly and honed his attention from the charred and lifeless body of the soldier towards Edmund, who was now on his knees, screaming for mercy.

"And so," I said, stepping forward. "We meet again!"

He looked at me with surprise, yet no disdain could I discern on this occasion, only terror, the greatest terror a man may witness when he is within a hair's breadth of certain death from the flames of a dragon.

Tan-y-Mynedd glared at Edmund and his eyes shone with a ferocity I had never seen in him before.

"Kill him!" Carron proffered an ideal solution as he flew around Edmund's head. "Have an end to it, and then we can eat him!"

"Wait, my friend. Wait!" I shouted. "An idea comes to my mind which is far better than killing him."

"You are being sentimental, Crach," Tan-y-Mynedd suggested.

Edmund looked frantically in all directions for help which would not be forthcoming.

"Very well, Crach," the dragon relaxed a little. "What is

this idea?"

I looked at Edmund and felt a pang of guilt for what I was about to suggest and just maybe, I did want to see him suffer more than I wanted him dead.

"The young dragon will wake within a couple of hours. I presume you will be able to take him back to the lair?" I questioned.

"I will," replied Tan-y-Mynedd, lowering his head and looking a little less fierce, but not much!

"As for you, Edmund!" I turned and stared at him. "What could be more embarrassing for you than to carry on with your life, enjoying your King's wrath?"

"What do you mean?" He looked petrified.

"It is simple, my old enemy, very simple indeed. I mean you must explain to your King how you managed to not catch a dragon so many had seen, explain why both of your henchmen are dead, one at the bottom of a bog and the other burned to charcoal by a dragon! How on earth will you explain all this when you remember nothing at all?"

"Of course, I will remember, Dwarf. Are you totally devoid of intellect? There is nothing wrong with my memory," he said, defensively.

"Are you sure about that?" I questioned.

"I am!" Edmund looked from me to the dragon and back again, as Carron continued to circle around our heads. "Of course, I am!"

Tan-y-Mynedd smiled, as only he can, noting the direction which my conversation with Edmund was heading. There was no need for any words between us and Carron squawked in all-knowing agreement, still circling around our heads.

Edmund staggered where he stood, a look of abject horror spread across his face as Tan-y-Mynedd sneezed a cloud of green smoke. Edmund quickly fell asleep and would sleep for hours now, softly in the swamp, and when he awoke later, he would have the 'mother of all headaches' and absolutely no memory of anything that had taken place.

Lord Edmund lay in the mud, snoring. Gathering the sleeping young dragon in his huge talons, Tan-y-Mynedd waited whilst I climbed on his back and held on tightly as he took flight, returning us safely to Ffestiniog, with Carron in pursuit.

I wondered how Edmund would talk his way out of this one!

CHAPTER THIRTY

We managed to return the young dragon to the others in the lair at Ffestiniog without further incident. Tan-y-Mynedd began again in earnest to teach the youngsters the ways of a dragon, ably assisted by my three dear friends, Faerydae, Fwynedd and Crow.

I returned to Sycharth and Owain howled with laughter when I relayed the Edmund saga. Owain remarked how there could be no better satisfaction than embarrassing another to the point of total tomfoolery, certainly more than dispatching them to another world by the blade. How Edmund would ever talk his way out of this was impossible to imagine, but whatever happened, one thing was certain, he would now have totally fallen from grace and arguably, it would be difficult, if not impossible, for him ever to regain the King's favour.

"On another matter, Crach. I have heard from Rhys ap Tudur and his brother, Gwilym. As we already know, they took the Castle at Conwy without so much as a drop of blood being shed. Sadly, that is no longer the case," Owain said.

"What do you mean, my Lord?" I asked.

"Hotspur attacked the Castle but was repelled and lost many men in the process. He told Rhys they were all guilty of treason and would be executed accordingly, so they may as well surrender. Rhys, of course, defended our honour and refused them. We are told that Hotspur has returned to London to seek the King's council," Owain replied.

"It is a good job we forged the supply needs on those letters to the King. Now our men should have enough food and water, as well as arrows, to hold out for some time yet," I added.

"We will not make this easy for the English at all, Crach, but I must see what we can do to assist my cousins, the Tudur's of Anglesey," Owain continued. "We did very well at Pumlumon, Crach, even though we were vastly outnumbered."

"Yes, my Lord, but the strategy was sound and the conditions were in our favour," I observed.

"Well, this year has gone better than we first thought it would," Owain commented.

"It has, my Lord, but we are still somewhat fragmented and our forces do need to unite around the country. Llwyd ap Crachan Llwyd informed me when he last visited, the unity we require will be achieved by the first month of the next year."

"Your old Master suggests we will be united by 1402?" Owain warmed his feet in front of the fire.

"Yes, my Lord."

"So, some months hence yet? We will see!" Owain called for food. We were both quite hungry.

*****

The King, together with the Lords of Essex, Lancaster and Lincoln, sat discussing the 'Welsh problem', as Henry now called the rebellion. Things were not going too well for them at all. King Henry's army had been smashed at the Battle of Mynydd Hyddgen and now the Tudur brothers held Conwy Castle.

Although he recruited Flemish mercenaries to join his own solders in Pembroke, the union was a disaster with a distinct lack of discipline and no commitment to the task in hand. Glyndwr's guerrilla tactics had won the day at Mynydd Hyddgen, which continued to be a huge embarrassment for Henry. Despite the Welsh being outnumbered by more than three to one, they had still critically immobilised his army by sound tactical decisions and strong discipline which was an important feature lacking in his own soldiery. And now, the embarrassment of the siege of Conway Castle to take on the chin. This was all just too much for King Henry!

The Tudur brothers, together with forty men, had captured and were defending Conwy Castle against Henry Percy 'Hotspur' and he had failed miserably in his attempt to retake it and arrest them all for high treason. So, the sentence of execution could not be carried out as the Welsh had defied all endeavours thus far for Hotspur to alter the balance in favour of his King. Henry was, to say the least, livid.

After Lancaster broke the news about Edmund's failure with the dragons, Henry flew into a rage of anger and confusion. He summoned Erasmus for guidance and Essex had to remind the King that Erasmus was, in fact, dead!

"Majesty," a page entered the room. "My Lord Henry Percy has arrived from Wales and awaits your pleasure."

Hotspur could not have arrived at a more inopportune time for himself. The King was in turmoil and at moments like this, his behaviour was most unpredictable. Hotspur was totally unaware of this as he was shown into the hall.

Confronted by The King, together with Lords seated at table, Henry Percy bowed his head with as much dignity that his embarrassment regarding the siege of Conwy Castle would allow. Hotspur had no choice but to suspend the attack. Although the Castle was defended by just forty men, not hundreds, it was a futile endeavour. Henry held no concern for details, only interested in results and he wasn't getting any of those. August 1401 was not a good month for the King of England and Hotspur was about to find out that it was not a good month for him either.

"So, Hotspur. The Tudurs are still in my Castle at Conwy and you have failed in the simple task I gave you. Why?" Henry was attempting to conceal his rage as best he could, but his anger was obvious to all those present.

"My Lord Percy, your King awaits an explanation," Lancaster leaned forward in a prosecutorial way, eying Hotspur closely.

Hotspur needed to contain his frustration. He had been there and witnessed the slaughter of his men with his own eyes, whilst the King and these fine Lords sat in judgment on matters they knew absolutely nothing about. Conwy Castle was impregnable when the English held it, so why would anything be different now just because it was held in the hands of the Welsh. The Castle was overflowing with supplies and the siege by the Tudur brothers at such a time seemed to him to be more than coincidence. This siege had been well planned in many ways.

"Your King awaits an explanation!" Henry tapped his fingers tunelessly on the table.

"Highness," Hotspur bowed again. "We will not take the Castle without siege engines, nor without being prepared to lose many more men."

"Rubbish!" Lancaster interrupted. "There are merely forty holding off hundreds of our men. I don't believe it!"

Remembering the bodies of his men piled high with arrows piercing into eyes and necks, Hotspur could not control his anger and stood his ground. "You speak of knowing that which you do not. Of seeing that which your eyes have not seen. You offend me, as you offend the dead, Lancaster. I advise you to shut your mouth if you know what is good for you!"

Lancaster rose from his seat. "You, Sir, are the one here to answer the King's questions, not I!" He sat down again.

"Now, get on with it, Hotspur!" Henry demanded.

Recognising the hopelessness of the position he was in, Hotspur began to explain the situation to the best of his ability. "I have told you of our needs, our expectations of success and the cost to our men. The Welsh will not surrender one life to execution and they see our actions as a crime of high treason against the Welsh Prince, Owain Glyndwr. So, my Lord, they do to us what we would do to them. I also fear that Glyndwr may take a large force to bolster them. We would be trapped between them at our rear and the Castle at our front."

Henry listened attentively and despite his previous thoughts, could see reason behind Hotspur's words.

Lancaster, on the other hand, saw things differently. "These are excuses for failure, not plans for success, Hotspur!"

he challenged again. "To consider the King to have committed high treason against Glyndwr is a joke, Sir, and you are the only clown in this circus."

"How dare you!" Hotspur retaliated.

"Enough!" Henry asserted himself as King. "We will reconsider and you, Lancaster, will be quiet!"

Lancaster looked peeved but knew better than to challenge the King in circumstances such as these. Looking down at the table, he averted his gaze from Hotspur's eyes.

"So, Hotspur, if they will not surrender themselves, we have no choice but to take the Castle. There is no point in negotiating if there is no need, and they have already proved such. So, you will return to Conway and take that Castle at all costs. Siege engines will be sent from Chester and you will have the men you require, no matter what the cost. Now, get out and do not enter my presence again until their heads are on spikes. Go, while I still have a mind to believe you," demanded Henry.

"My Lord," Hotspur bowed and reversed himself from the King's presence. "As you command."

Riding back to Wales, his heart was not filled with hope. Even with more men and siege engines being transported from Chester, many were bound to fall in this onslaught of the Castle and Henry held no mind to it. Hotspur's thoughts were as grey and cloudy as the sky above and it was imperative he found a way to negotiate with the Tudurs, hundreds of men's lives depended on it, irrespective of the King's command.

Chapter Thirty-One

Edmund awoke from the longest sleep he had ever slept and with a headache that felt like thunder clapping deep inside his skull. Never had he experienced a headache like this before. It was like the mother of all hangovers, yet he could not remember having had any ale, or wine even. In fact, he could remember nothing at all!

Cold and damp from sleeping in the mud and filthy from head to toe, Edmund slowly sat up and looked around. The remnants of a smashed wagon and cage strewn across the bog drew his attention and then his eyes fell upon the many horse carcasses laying on the hillside. What was this place? What was he doing here? Edmund searched his mind but could find no answers. The last thing he could remember was sitting in a tavern, but he could not recall anything that happened afterwards or even why he was there in the first place. And, oh, how his head ached!

Within the fog of his mind, Edmund vaguely remembered searching endlessly for dragons that did not exist, a quest given to him by the King. He did remember hoping that if such a creature did exist and he could catch or kill one, it would restore his place in the King's favour. He also recalled being in the company of two companions, but where were they? Why was he now alone? Why was he here on this God-forsaken mountainside?

The more faint memories returned, the more his head ached, but there were no memories of dragon encounters to recall. Those memories had gone up in green smoke, but, of course, he didn't remember that either. Now he was alone, not even knowing where he was or, indeed, what he should do now.

Bedraggled and somewhat a shadow of his former self, Edmund was confused, his clothes ragged and torn, all the usual finery gone. He rose to rather shaky feet, gathered himself and began to walk down the mountainside to, hopefully, find a town with a tavern. He did hold a brief recollection in the mists of memory, there was one not too far away.

When Edmund walked through the door of the tavern, Sam Hetherington recognised the once brash and vulgar Edmund for what he was, rather than who he saw now. Edmund stood at the counter, still a little hungover and with a blinding headache, leaning against it for support.

"You look as if you have been in the wars, Sir," Sam remarked innocently but not without cause, given Edmund's appearance.

"I need a room with a bath, Landlord, and I would like you to fetch me some clean clothes," Edmund stated.

"I can do that, Sir, but the clothes will not be up to your usual finery, I am afraid." Sam scratched his chin with a grubby fat finger. "If you would take a seat, Sir, I will bring hot wine to warm you and a little food perhaps?"

Edmund was starving, it felt as if he had not eaten for at least a month. Excessive hunger is also another unfortunate side effect of the 'dragon's green smoke', but Edmund would not know anything about that either.

"Thank you." Edmund was much more reserved than his usual self and quietly said, "I will sit here and eat by the fire and then perhaps I may take my bath?"

"Yes. Yes, of course. I will bring you wine, together with bread and cheese for now to stave your hunger." Sam disappeared into the kitchen and Edmund sat by the warmth of the fire. He knew something was not right, but just could not put a finger on the source of his disquiet.

Edmund felt a little better after he had eaten and had enjoyed a good soak in a hot bath, but his head still ached and he was still bothered by a lack of memory, fearing he had forgotten something very important, which, of course, was true. Sitting by the fire in the tavern with Sam fussing about him was a welcome change from the cold of the mountainside and Edmund was beginning to feel more like his old self. He hailed Sam for more wine.

"Straight away, Sir," Sam complied, rushing over with a jug, he replenished Edmund's goblet.

"More wood on the fire, I think, don't you?" Neglecting to thank Sam for the wine. Edmund had returned to giving orders, his recent experience having not served to humble his manners in the slightest.

"I will be staying tonight but I will leave at first light and shall have need of a horse."

"Yes, my Lord," Sam bowed appropriately.

Edmund tossed a gold coin to Sam, who caught it between deft fingers.

The following morning, Lord Edmund rose as the cock crowed. He took a breakfast of porridge and eggs before paying his final bill, much to Sam's surprise. Dressed in clothes not befitting his station in life, Edmund collected a horse from the stable and rode out into the sunshine. It was going to be a fine day, clear blue skies, with no wind to speak of as Edmund began his journey to Hotspur in the north. He dare not return to London because the last thing he remembered was being on a quest 'searching for dragons', but that was all he could recall, apart from the King's words, forbidding him to return unless he caught or killed the alleged beast. Going to see Hotspur may, perhaps, be of some help, Edmund thought to himself. This was certainly a better option than a visit to the King!

He knew nothing of the battle of Mynedd Hyddgen, nor the siege of Conwy Castle and, of course, these events were slightly more important to Hotspur than Edmund's predicament which essentially boiled down to him losing two men, his memory and favour with the King.

Ever hopeful he would find a way to get out of the mire he was in, Edmund rode on.

CHAPTER THIRTY-TWO

"How is he now?" I asked Tan-y-Mynedd.

The great dragon paused before he answered, "The poppy juice wore off eventually and he is none the worse for the experience. There are no injuries but his attitude concerns me greatly. He has a bloodlust, Crach!"

This was not good news, a dragon with a bloodlust is a dangerous thing to behold. I fully understood his concerns and shivered inside from head to toe at the thought of such a thing.

"It was the feeding on horse carcasses and, I think, he has tasted human flesh, Crach, in fact, of that I am certain." Tan-y-Mynedd shook his huge head in disbelief. "Sadly, I have killed a few men over the years and, of course, very recently, I killed Edmund's man, but I have never tasted their flesh.

When a dragon gets a taste of it, a bloodlust for human flesh can become an obsession to the point of madness, Crach, and this is my fear. If madness overcomes him, we will not be able to control him. Faerydae made a potion which she managed to get down him eventually, but not before he spat it out several times."

Here was yet another crisis we had not seen coming and one of a grave magnitude indeed.

"I hope my fears will not be realised," Tan-y-Mynedd explained. "But throughout our ancient history, I have never known of a good outcome when a bloodlust occurs, although I do know it always ends in grief." He shook his head again. "The only other incident like this I remember, was when I was about four years old and one of the older dragons contracted a full-blown bloodlust. After being attacked by men, he tasted their flesh while defending himself. There was no real difference in his behaviour at first, but within a month or two, he would disappear at all hours to who knows where. We would hear stories of raids on distant villages and learned he would fly down and attack for no real reason. This was a dragon intoxicated with a human bloodlust. He would ignite their homes with his flame and as the people fled, would catch and devour them. This went on for about two years, but he was eventually hunted down by the villagers, who posted rewards for his death. They managed to corner him on the Black Mountain in the south where the great dragon was slain, but he took many lives before they finally killed him. It was horrendous, Crach, and it affected every other dragon. You see, it only takes one dragon to make an enemy of all men and all dragons become bound up in a cycle of hatred. Despite the fact this was over three hundred years ago, to me, it is as if it was yesterday. When you witness such things, they stain your memory forever." Again, he shook his head in resignation.

"Is there anything that can be done?" I asked.

"Well, if the potion Faerydae made does not work, the short answer is, no." A flick of this tail dislodged some rock which fell to the cave floor. "He will have to be curtailed in some way. The less he eats, the more hungry and unpredictable he will become. He already lusts for blood and, unfortunately, sheep will not satisfy him."

Fwynedd walked into the chamber. "He is sleeping. A draught of Faerydae's potion has done its work."

"The idea, for the time-being, is if we can keep him asleep for a while, he will wake up hungry enough to eat a sheep," Faerydae suggested. "I have to wean him off human flesh."

"Is that even possible?" I asked.

"I don't know," she replied. "It just seems to make good sense to me, but I do have to keep him asleep. The longer he is away from the idea of human flesh, it might, hopefully, help him to forget about it but, to be honest, I cannot be certain this will work. Bloodlust is something which I have never heard of being cured before. In fact, quite the opposite but, we can only try."

"And, what of the others?" I enquired.

"We dragons are sensitive creatures," Tan-y-Mynedd said. "What one may feel, we all sense, of that there is no doubt. Some, in particular, are badly affected by this, sensing the unrest in spirit, but all of them are aware of the changes he is experiencing. There is definitely disquiet and a certain amount of confusion amongst them. They are still very young and inexperienced so we cannot expect them to easily deal with this, especially so soon after the grief of losing three of their brothers crushed in the caves. It is very difficult for them. We need to bring a sense of calm but whilst-ever he is still as he is, the disquiet in their spirits will continue. So, to keep him asleep will be the best thing to enable the others to feel more peaceful and less disturbed."

"This is my reason for using Valerian tincture," Faerydae interjected.

"I hope this works for all our sakes," I expressed. I held a lot of faith in Faerydae but this was a very difficult problem, even for her. She had wonderful skills as a healer and when the dragons were very young and seriously ill, she saved their lives with her intuition. She is, indeed, very special, being so blessed. She holds a place in my heart, but I am not sure if she knows that. "Maybe she does, Crach!" Tan-y-Mynedd disturbed my thoughts. Then laughed.

I felt the blood rise to my neck and I must have turned the colour of beetroot. This dragon had, once again, 'heard my mind'. I decided to laugh it off but Faerydae wanted to know what we were both so amused by.

"Nothing at all!" I said. This made Tan-y-Mynedd really boom with laughter.

"What is he laughing at now?" she questioned, looking quite confused.

"I know not," I answered. "Who could ever understand the mind of a dragon, it certainly defeats me!" I smiled and she appeared to shrug off the 'need to know', which was indeed a great relief to me.

The young dragons were growing by the day and starting to need food less often which gave Fwynedd more time to relax. They also slept for longer. Tan-y-Mynedd spent several hours each day, teaching them in the ways of the dragon and in the dead of night, he would take them to the outside world to fly, while the dragon suffering from bloodlust slept on.

This was a very busy time for all of us and there was no sign of any let-up for quite a while yet, but all seemed to be under control, at least for now.

For me, Crach Ffinnant, dwarf, prophet and seer, there was much to do.

CHAPTER THIRTY-THREE

Edmund rode into Hotspur's encampment near to the Castle in Conwy an hour ago but Hotspur was out elsewhere, probably trying to plan ways of getting the Tudur brothers and the rebels out of the Castle. As usual, Edmund thought everyone should be at his beck and call and arrogantly showed his frustration to others. He sat in the tavern which had been erected by the army, quaffing ale and making snide remarks to any who may be within hearing distance.

A soldier stood at the bar and took offence at Edmund's manner. "Just because you think you are special, don't mean you are, you posh ponce!" the soldier said as he slammed his tankard on the bar. "You might be a lord, but you can still bleed!"

"How dare you speak to me in that fashion? I have the

King's ear!" Edmund responded with a hint of superiority, not noticing Henry Percy had walked in with Constable Massy and was now standing quietly behind him.

"You have what?" stormed Hotspur, interrupting the conversation.

"The King's ear," Edmund replied emphatically, turning around to see where the voice came from. Upon seeing Henry Percy, his arrogance subsided a little, but not by much. "Ah, Lord Percy! It is you! Good day. I trust I find you in good health?" Edmund grovelled, all previous anger towards the soldier now fading in importance.

"Edmund, why are you here rather than about the King's business?" Hotspur looked at Massy and said, "I don't have time for this fool."

"No, my Lord," Massy agreed. "There are more pressing matters to be dealt with."

"Very well, Edmund. Come to my tent in half an hour and I will listen to you," Hotspur suggested with a degree of resignation.

"But I have little time!" Edmund attempted to assert himself. "Surely you can see me now. I have travelled a long way."

"Then, I suggest you use this half-hour to rest further after your long journey, Edmund, and have a care, Sir, do not try my patience and leave my men alone. Do I make myself clear?"

Edmund, as usual when defeated, backed down with a scowl.

Half an hour later, Constable Massy arrived back at the makeshift tavern and escorted Edmund to Henry Percy. As the tent flap opened and the two men stepped in, Henry Percy took control of the interview immediately because, in his mind, it would be short, sharp and to the point. "Ah, Lord Edmund, come in and take a seat. Tell me what you want and make it quick!" Hotspur asserted. "I have no time for your incessant moaning."

"I would heed his Lordship, if I were you, Lord Edmund," Massy advised in a low voice.

Edmund stayed silent but glared at Massy with incredulity. How dare he speak to him like this, but he thought it best not to air his anger. He knew his place, even though he thought all others, including present company, should have a trifle more respect for him. He so desired to be at a higher station in life than sadly he found himself in at the moment. Edmund bit his lip and refrained from commenting. Hotspur was not a man to be messed with, his reputation went before him.

"So, Edmund," Hotspur reminded him by tone of voice, time was precious. "What have you to say?"

"I would crave your indulgence, my Lord," requested Edmund.

"You have it. Stop grovelling man!" Hotspur retaliated with a hint of venom in his voice.

"I have lost my two guards!" Edmund stumbled over his words.

"You have what?" Hotspur could not hide his surprise in hearing the word 'lost' within the context of his words. He shuffled in his seat, clearly agitated by Edmund's presence.

"I have lost my men," Edmund repeated. "I have no guard, Sir!" he pleaded.

"A Lord who loses his men does not deserve to have any. How do you lose two men?" Hotspur could not believe what he was hearing.

"I do not know what happened because I cannot remember!" Edmund retaliated.

"And that is an excuse?" Hotspur rounded on Edmund. "Are you a buffoon, Sir?"

Lord Edmund was furious at the accusation but he daren't show it.

"You come here, demand my time and tell me you have LOST your men. Are you completely deranged, Sir? You waste my time with the ramblings of a lunatic." Hotspur poured himself a goblet of wine, he needed something to anesthetise himself from this diatribe. Edmund made him despair, never had he known such a coward. Hotspur had spent hours trying to negotiate with Rhys ap Tudur, a man for whom he held in the highest regard, and witnessed the deaths of over two hundred of his men at the point of Welsh arrows and now— now he was wasting his time and intelligence listening to this. "Listen to me, Edmund, and hear my words well. You come here attempting to get me to intercede with the King on your behalf. Are you a complete fool, Sir?"

Edmund stared at the ground, unable to look at Henry Percy.

"Let me tell you, I am negotiating for the lives of brave men, men who you are not fit to lick the boots of, and they are Welshmen. Do you hear me? My negotiations with the King are about saving lives and serving justice. Neither of which mean anything to you, do they?"

Massy looked frustrated. Edmund was an idiot and a privileged one at that.

"So, Edmund, what do you expect now? You are out of favour, my friend. The King cares not to hear more excuses. You have failed again." He sipped some wine. "You had best return to your mission and find those dragons or you will be sure to lose your head. The King is adamant."

Edmund turned as pale as cows' milk and a slight tremor

spread through his body. The idea of losing his head did not appeal to him in the slightest!

"Edmund, I have nothing else to say. Do you?" Hotspur enquired.

It was clear to Edmund he was wasting his time pleading with Hotspur. He would get no help here, but perhaps one last try. "At least could you let me have a couple of men?" Edmund was almost grovelling now.

"You can have one man, but don't come back for another if you lose him!" Hotspur told him, sarcastically. "Constable Massy, will you organise this please?"

"My Lord," Massy affirmed, with a bow of his head. "Lord Edmund, if you will follow me?" He raised the tent flap, inviting Edmund to leave. The meeting was over.

Hotspur drained his goblet while watching Edmund leave, relieved he was gone.

"He has a man now?" Hotspur asked Massy as he re-entered the tent five minutes later.

"Yes, my Lord, and I gave him a fresh horse, supplies and clothes, then sent him on his way," Massy replied.

"Thank the saviour for that!" Hotspur exclaimed. "I hope I have seen the last of him but somehow, I don't think I have."

"What of the rebels, Sir?" enquired Constable Massy.

"Well, I have negotiated with them and, finally, Rhys ap Tudur has agreed that eight of his men will be given up for execution in the morning. We will collect them from the Castle and Fellows will escort them to Chester where the King intends to hang, draw and quarter them in the public square."

Massy did not like Fellows and neither did Hotspur. He was not unlike Edmund in his arrogance and was so full of self-importance. A weasel of a man, tall and thin with sharp features, wispy hair and spots over his forehead. Fellows had not seen battle to date, yet held the King's ear as a spy against Hotspur. Henry IV did not trust anybody but, like Edmund, Fellows did his bidding without question and always at the expense of others. Hotspur attended meetings with him, as instructed by the King, and he had been discourteously rude on several occasions during negotiations with the rebels. Rhys ap Tudur suggested to Hotspur, he put Fellows in front of the army in the morning and he could ensure an arrow would permanently put an end to the man's arrogance and disrespect. Hotspur thanked Rhys but diplomatically refused the offer. Anyway, he would be taking the army north after the garrison was re-established at Conwy Castle, whilst Massy returned to the castle and Fellows accompanied the condemned rebels to Chester, taking with him a hundred men for protection.

"I will take an early night, Constable Massy," he said. "Tomorrow, Conwy Castle is ours again."

CHAPTER THIRTY-FOUR

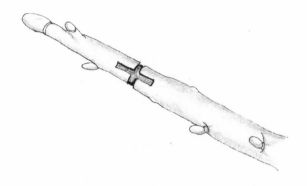

Rhys and Gwilym ap Tudur stood by the gates of Conwy Castle, waiting for the English to arrive. Gwilym, together with seven of their men, had drawn sticks carved with a cross last night. A total of forty-two men chose a stick each from a bag and those who picked the eight selected would now face the King's executioner in Chester, as agreed with Hotspur.

"Don't concern yourself, Gwilym," Rhys tried to offer some reassurance. "I am happy, as your older brother, to take your place."

"You will not! This is the way it must be. Although I am not full of the joys of spring, this is not the kind of death I had in mind for myself. It is a death of farce."

The brothers embraced and Rhys held Gwilym in a bear-like hug, squeezing the breath from him.

"We will do what we can," Rhys said, trying to dilute the gravity of the situation facing them.

In less than one hour, Fellows and Constable Massy would ride across the drawbridge to accept the surrender of the Castle and eight rebels would be taken, despatched to Chester by wagon and executed, as a lesson to all others. Henry originally wanted all of the rebels' lives but after prolonged negotiations, just eight Welshmen had been agreed upon, much to the disgust of the Tudur brothers but, in reality, they had no choice. Starvation was the only alternative outcome if they did not agree to terms. The English had surrounded the Castle with no intention of letting the Welsh leave.

Now, the moment had arrived. One of the rebels announced the English were riding across the drawbridge which Rhys lowered earlier in preparation for this dreadful juncture.

Fellows sat astride a warhorse, clad in armour ill-fitted to a man with a frame such as his. His sallow complexion and thin emaciated face was almost lost under his armour and he appeared most ungainly astride a horse. If ever a man looked out of place in a situation, this was it.

Constable John Massy awaited the command to enter the Castle which had been his home until the Welsh seized it. Now he was returning.

"Rhys ap Tudur! This is Master Fellows, the King's agent, and I command you to open the gates." Fellows hailed the rebel soldiers on the battlements. His attitude was aggressive and arrogant.

Rhys fumed quietly under his breath. "Open the gates!" Rhys ordered. The huge wooden gate creaked open and the English retinue, led by Fellows and Massy, rode into the

Castle courtyard.

"Bind them!" ordered Fellows, pointing to the eight men who stood in a group with Rhys, the unfortunate ones who had drawn the sticks carved with a cross from the bag last night. "Bind them and chain all to the wagon." Fellows dismounted and faced Rhys.

"So, your brother will die!" Fellows joked sarcastically. "At last, the King will see at least one of you Tudur scum in quarters!"

It was all Rhys could do not to kill Fellows where he stood, the man was intolerable and demonstrated very little dignity.

"Get them in the wagon, now!" he reiterated. It was obvious he felt very uncomfortable and needed to get this unenviable task behind him.

Gwilym ap Tudur joined his comrades as they climbed aboard the wagon and were chained tightly to each other with rusty manacles by the guards.

"Get a move on, scum!" The guards manhandled them into place on the wagon.

Rhys and the others could do nothing except watch their comrades being abused.

Constable Massy gave instructions to his men and the King's command of two hundred soldiers became the new garrison of Conwy Castle. Some busied themselves searching every corner of the castle to ensure no surprises lurked as the Welsh were about to leave.

"Move it! Move it!" Fellows bellowed commands, clearly out of his depth in this setting, and looking quite comical in his armour. Rhys could not help but grin at the sight of him, but he and his men stood and watched with sadness and compassion as the wagon, pulled by four oxen, carried their comrades, including Rhys's brother, out of the Castle and across the drawbridge, their destination, Chester and execution.

When Rhys and his men rode out of the Castle, they were jeered and cajoled by the English town folk, but they fared better than those in the wagon who were bombarded with rotten fruit and eggs, but at least they were all alive, for the moment.

Thomas Easton stood in the shadows of the Castle, watching the Welsh leave. They had been kind to him and he had learned a fair bit of their language too. Now they were gone and replaced by the new garrison who were busying themselves with their duties. Unseen, Thomas sneaked as quietly as a mouse down through a gap in the castle wall to the water's edge and slipped into the moat, swimming to the far bank where he climbed out and disappeared into the night.

Rhys and his men rode north with the intention of following the wagon at a safe distance until they could think of a plan to free their comrades. It would need to be a very good one as Gwilym and the others were heavily guarded. Outriders from Rhys's band kept their eyes on Fellows and the English while they stayed well hidden and camouflaged.

Unbeknown to Rhys and the others, Thomas Easton had met up with some of Glyndwr's men and a plot was being hatched.

***

Thomas lay on the track in the mud, bruised and beaten. Fellows, riding at the front of the column, was the first to see the body lying prostrate on the ground. Fellows raised his hand. "Hold!" he commanded. The procession of English, together with the wagon holding eight rebels in chains, ground to a halt. "See to him!" Ordered Fellows. Two riders dismounted to examine Thomas Easton. One of them took hold of him by the shoulder, turning him over. A blood-stained and bruised face stared back up at them, only half-conscious but still breathing.

"He is beaten badly, Sir, but not dead," one of the riders shouted. "He will live."

Due to the unforeseen hold-up, Fellows ordered the men to dismount and to rest whilst he questioned this man found on the road. The riders made Thomas as comfortable as possible and gave him water to drink, reviving his consciousness.

"Oh, thank you. Thank you. I thought I would die!" Thomas gasped.

"Who did this to you, man?" Fellows questioned.

"Welsh rebels, Sir. It was Welsh rebels," came his reply.

"But why, man?" Fellows pursued the point.

"I overheard them nattering and they caught me, Sir." Thomas looked up at Fellows with fear in his eyes.

"Overheard what?" Fellows' ears pricked, he needed to know more.

"They were talking about an ambush, Sir. I think possibly of your party but I know not for sure. There was mention of a wagon and prisoners. It is hard to remember with any accuracy," he said, holding his head. "My head aches." Thomas's left eye was swollen and a bruise spread from his chin to his ear, blue and purple.

"They beat you?" Fellows asked.

"Yes, Sir," Thomas stuttered. "I was beaten so I would forget what I heard."

"And what did you hear?" Fellows now gave his full attention to this man. "You are an Englishman, are you not?"

"I am, Sir. From Chester," Thomas replied.

"And what did you hear?" Fellows repeated his earlier question.

"I cannot say, they will kill me if they find out," Thomas pleaded, but Fellows simply replied coldly.

"And I will kill you if you don't tell me what you heard."

Thomas looked into Fellows' eyes and knew he meant every word.

"They spoke about two routes to Flint. One said you would take the inland route rather than the coastal one and they would ambush you south of Flint."

"Oh, they did, did they?" Fellows smiled when he thought he could get one over on the rebels. All he had to do was to take the coastal route. "Good! Put him in the wagon," Fellows ordered the Captain of the Guard, informing him the party would be altering their route and taking the coastal paths instead.

"But that may be difficult for the wagon to pass over, Sir," suggested the Captain.

"We will do as I say. The rebels lay in wait for us inland."

"Yes, Sir!" the Captain accepted the orders but he was aware of this route and suspected Thomas may have been planted with the intention of misleading them, but when he suggested this to Fellows, he would not hear of such a thing and dismissed him to go and redirect the procession as ordered.

As the riders assisted Thomas into the back of the wagon, his eyes met with Gwilym's. They knew each other from Conwy Castle but something made Gwilym, and the others, fail to acknowledge him, as Thomas did them. He sat next to Gwilym with a blanket around his shoulders to keep him warm, unlike his fellow passengers who sat exposed to the elements.

When the wagon was underway, an opportunity arose when nobody was watching or listening for the two men to whisper to each other.

Gwilym was the first to speak. "What are you doing here, Thomas, and how did you get beaten so badly. Did the English do this to you?"

"No, my Lord, it is a ruse to make them change their route so you can be rescued. Your brother follows behind but Glyndwr waits ahead." He smiled warmly.

"Ah," Gwilym said requiring no further explanation.

As the wagon rattled on, the driver hurled abuse after abuse with backward glances at the prisoners. "Nothing like a good hanging!" He shouted. "You get cut down before you die, see! A big bucket of cold water gets chucked over your head to bring you back and then, guess what?" He paused for effect. "A big sharp knife slides from yer groin to yer breastbone so all yer innards drop out!" He laughed. "Then they burn em in front of your eyes and chop you up!"

"He is a bastard," Thomas whispered to Gwilym.

"He has not stopped abusing us since we left Conwy," Gwilym replied.

Fellows headed up the column again with little caution in his mind, thinking he had outwitted the rebels. In his thoughts, it was most fortuitous to stumble upon the Englishman, lying beaten in the mud. How nice it was to be one step ahead.

Rounding the bluff, Fellows was greeted by a most unexpected sight. A row of fifty Welsh archers with longbows stood poised for attack. Fellows called the troop to a halt when more archers appeared on each side of them. Then he saw a rider approaching from the north at a gallop, skidding to a halt not one hundred paces away.

It was Emrys. "Surrender and hand over your prisoners, or else die. The choice is all yours." Emrys raised his broadsword. "When I lower this sword, you all die!"

Unsure of what to do, Fellows looking rather scared, turned to the Captain for reassurance. It was, after all, a real fight and he was most vulnerable with no experience of battle. This was not a game and he could lose his life, and lose it soon!

"It's a trap, Sir!" The Captain took account of the rebels to the fore and at each side of his men. There was no cover to speak of and his entire troop was surrounded on three sides. They could not turn the wagon around on the narrow track with a sheer drop to one side. They could surrender or, if foolish, fight. Looking at Fellows, he suggested surrender, but Fellows would not hear of it. The Captain made further protestations but Fellows raised his sword with some difficulty due to his lack of physical strength and hailed a charge. The Captain could do naught but comply as the troops behind him did likewise, following Fellows in a full-frontal charge. Bowmen on either side of them let loose cedar bows and arrows rained down on Fellows and his men. Many fell to the ground, dead or wounded in the first hail of arrows which was quickly followed by a second when yet more fell. Fellows rode on, oblivious to the carnage behind him when, suddenly, he was aware of a knight in armour, sporting the insignia of Glyndwr. The knight sat tall on a charger, looking strong and well-seasoned in battle, appearing intent on bringing down this arrogant Englishman who was riding towards him. Fellows recognised the knight and was instantly filled with a fear that spread through every cell in his gangly frame. He had previously seen him at Court, this was Owain Glyndwr he was about to do battle with! Adrenaline pumped through his veins and he tried to raise his sword to attack or defend, whichever might come first, but he lacked the strength. It was too late for him as their horses crashed. Glyndwr's mount reared on impact and its hooves knocked Fellows to the ground. He fell heavily and as he struggled to get up, a sharp clout at the back of his head put him back down again.

"My Lord," Emrys bowed to Owain whilst holding his horse's reins in one hand and the hammer that put Fellows on the ground in the other.

"Thank you, Emrys." Owain dismounted. "Who is this fool?" He bent down, removing Fellows' visor, pulling his head back to get a good look at the face beneath. "I know this weasel," Owain remarked. "This is Fellows, the King's spy and he still lives. Bind him Emrys."

In no time, the English escort of one hundred men were mostly dead or wounded. All those not dead, including Fellows, were chained and took the places of the Welsh in the wagon. The captain died needlessly when an arrow pierced his throat and when he fell from his horse, he was trampled under the mounts of those who followed behind.

An atmosphere of great success and victory spread amongst the Welsh as the prisoners were freed.

Gwilym bowed, respectfully to Owain. "My Lord. I owe you my life."

CHAPTER THIRTY-FIVE

I sat wondering how the imminent winter may turn out to be. Owain and his men were now, in essence, rebels and outlaws and we could not return to Sycharth, Glyndwr's home, as it was being watched. The English were hunting us incessantly across the land now and my Prince had a price on his head. Henry courted betrayal from all corners of Wales.

Here we were, camped in the forest and while we enjoyed warm accommodation in the specially constructed hideaway, snow was on the horizon. I watched Owain standing with his back to the fire, staring up at the stars with a look of concern on his face. We were now caught in a mist of deception.

A cold wind blew from the north and I shivered but had a feeling this was due to more than just the weather. I held an uneasy feeling and whilst I knew it had something to do with the dragons, I did not know exactly what it was. I simply had a great sense of foreboding.

A shadowy figure rode into camp and by the time he had dismounted, yet another visitor was arriving for this important meeting Owain had requested.

Tudur appeared in the company of Rhys and Gwilym, greeting Owain with smiles and firm handshakes. Since Rhys and Gwilym had been reunited following the ambush, they had joined Owain, along with their small band of forty men. The meeting began as those invited, including me, sat around the fire.

"Well, gentlemen, this is a good time for us to talk, is it not?" Owain suggested to all, with a broad grin stretching across his face.

"Brother," Tudur chirped up. "We are on a tide of change!"

"Indeed, Cousin!" agreed Rhys. "We have done well in every encounter thus far, considering how outnumbered we have been."

"Our tactics have worked well," Owain added. "We have used our terrain against them effectively, but it is only a matter of time before they also get accustomed to it."

"Perhaps." Tudur was a little concerned.

"Brother, why so negative. We have endured well." On seeing the concern in his eyes, Owain took Tudur by the arm to proffer comfort.

"It worries me that we are less than seven hundred against Henry's huge armies." Tudur raised his arms to the heavens. "We have been lucky so far!"

"We have out-fought them and out-thought them," Rhys added.

"Ever the poet!" his brother, Gwilym, chuckled but the smile soon left his face. "It was I that was going to be quartered at the King's pleasure."

Rhys laughed and said, "Yes, but you weren't, were you?"

"No, we got you out, didn't we?" Emrys asserted. "And we thrashed those arrogant Fellows and his men. Which reminds me, what are we going to do with him, ransom or kill?"

"Emrys," Rhys replied before anyone else had a chance. "We should kill him. He is Henry's lapdog!"

"He is worth coin," I chipped in.

"Yes, he is, Crach, and that is worthy of thought," Owain agreed.

"He is a selfish buffoon! I should kill him myself!" Gwilym leapt to his feet. "I was wronged by him more than anybody else was so I should be the one to dispose of him!"

"Hold fast, Gwilym," Owain gesticulated for him to sit down. "Be calm, no decision is yet made. Take some wine and relax. Emrys, pass him the flagon."

Emrys complied with his Prince's request, passing the flagon to Gwilym. "Thank you, my friend." Gwilym took the flagon, dispensing with the need of a goblet, he lifted it to dry parched lips and drank deeply. "I thought I was going to die, I really thought it was my end, we all did."

"Of course, we understand that," Rhys tried to support his brother. "It was the same for us, we did not know of Owain's plan. I thought I would lose my brother, but Gwilym and I rejoice that was not to be."

"We are all alive," I said. "For the moment, at least."

"There's cheerful, Crach!" mocked Tudur.

"I am a realist, my friends, and can make no apology for that." But they all knew me better than to think I would.

"Crach is correct. It is for the moment we are alive, but up against all of the force that is gathered under Henry's banner, it is only realistic to consider that it is only a matter of time," said Gwilym.

"Look," Owain defended his position. "I know we have had much on our side, but, nevertheless, we have still been victorious. Men will gather under our banner and we will rid Wales of the tyranny brought by the yoke of the usurper King. All is written in 'The Prophecy', is it not, Crach?"

He was correct, it is so written but the reality of the conflict thus far had seen over seventy Welshmen killed or very seriously wounded, of which nothing was written. I reminded him of Llwyd ap Crachan Llwyd's words. "We are told it will be the next year when all will rally under the banners of the dragon, my Lord."

"Next year!" Gwilym and Tudur both remarked in unison.

Tudur said, "We have to live long enough first, Brother, and I know we have done well, but imagine if they ever caught us on flat ground or, worse still, between the forces of Henry to the south and Hotspur to the north. We would be slaughtered!"

He was right, but whilst all these seeds of doubt were being sown, I recognised that 'The Prophecy' neither saw the death nor the capture of our Prince within its ancient words. Not one word indicated such an outcome existed.

"We are on the run now, like outlaws. We cannot go home and winter is ahead." Tudur drank from the goblet again, swallowing deeply while considering his next words carefully. "I know we will be fine in the forest, as we have everything we need." He looked thoughtfully into the fire then added. "Except women, of course! Don't you miss Margaret, Owain?"

"Of course, I do!" he was quick to reply. "I love my wife as I love my people, but choices are not mine to make."

Despite the recent successes of our rebellion against the English, we were now living as outlaws, hunted by the English in every corner of our country. Well, at least we were safe, for the time being.

"I think we should eat, drink and concentrate on making ourselves feel good, despite some of the things we have spoken about. It is only natural there is good and bad, that is the way of war, and, believe me, my friends, we are at war," said Owain.

"Quite right!" Rhys supported his cousin. "And at the moment, we are winning, no matter what some might think."

Gwilym took another long gulp from the flagon, burped loudly and said, "So, when do I get to kill Fellows?"

CHAPTER THIRTY-SIX

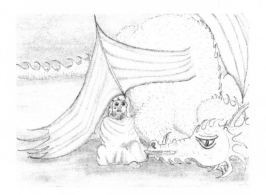

It was extremely cold this morning. The cock crowed about an hour ago as I was sitting down to breakfast. An early frost created a blanket of glittering kaleidoscopes in front of my eyes.

With a great flapping of wings, Carron the Raven suddenly landed on my shoulder. My heart almost stopped in shock! I mean, one moment I sit in a world of my own and the next, a raven drops from the sky, landing on my shoulder with the customary piercing of claws into flesh. My flesh! And, without a warning of any kind.

Gathering myself from the ripples of shock still coursing through my dwarfness, I took a deep breath and tried to regain my composure. "Carron! By dragon's breath! Surely an announcement of your arrival could be given! Perhaps a squawk of some kind may prevent my early retirement from this life, a demise as sure as sunrise, from shock". I emphasised my point. "Carron—shock!"

But it did not matter a jot to Carron. He preened his feathers, mindless to my words. He waited until I'd finished speaking, then, sticking his huge beak into my ear, he told me of some news I would rather not have heard. "Crach! Oh, Crach! The dragon with a bloodlust has gone again, but he has not left the lair on his own this time!"

"What do you mean?" I asked with great concern. "Not on his own?"

"Two of the others left with him. Tan-y-Mynedd is furious!" Carron continued. "It is awful, Crach. All of the others are very disturbed by what is happening and there is great unrest in the lair. Crow, of course, is feeling guilty for all the woes of the world, but especially for this. Nothing can be done to console him and, believe me, Faerydae has tried everything she knows."

"Has Tan-y-Mynedd gone in search of them?" I asked.

"He has, Crach," Carron answered.

"When did this happen, Carron?"

He looked very worried and you may think 'how can you tell when a raven is worried?' Well, the answer is, I cannot tell you. I just knew. Maybe it was something in his eyes or the way he ruffled his feathers, I know not.

"It was last night. I came to tell you as quickly as I could. There is mayhem in the lair, you know how sensitive dragons are to each other."

"Yes, I do," I replied.

This was not good news at all, in fact, it could not really be worse.

Carron pecked at my ear-ring, a pastime enjoyed by him

since the first day we met, and despised by me for years! It often hurt, but of that he was oblivious. It was almost as if he was saying 'Well, I can't feel a thing'. Ravens will be ravens as, indeed, dragons will be dragons. He flitted from my shoulder to drink from a pool of melted ice nearby.

This certainly was a major crisis. It was bad enough the young dragon had disappeared again, but much worse he had taken two of the others with him this time. It was really going to upset the apple cart in more ways than one. Where in the name of 'dragon's breath' could they be and why had two others followed him? Perhaps the youngsters were so sensitive to his anxiety and bloodlust, their curiosity got the better of them. Only time would tell, of course.

I asked Carron to return to the lair at Ffestiniog to check if Faerydae, Crow or Fwynedd needed my help. I had my own magical way to contact Tan-y-Mynedd. At no time in the past had I ever needed to use it, but this was different and a unique situation. This was an emergency. Digging deep into my bag, I pulled out a small leather wrap and from inside it, the ancient bone whistle, carved from a dragon's tooth. It had been carved many hundreds of years ago and given to me by Tan-y-Mynedd when I was still an apprentice to Llwyd ap Crachan Llwyd, my old Master, with strict instructions to only use it in extreme circumstances. Its purpose was to summon the dragon and demanded two things which were, this ancient whistle and a pure heart. I was fortunate to have both and for the first time in my life, I put it to my lips and blew five long blasts which I could not hear. The sound is inaudible to human ears as it is so high-pitched and beyond our capabilities. After the five blasts, I sat in wait, looking up into an empty sky.

I sat for over an hour, with my eyes looking upwards.

There were plenty of birds, hawks, even a bat or two, but no dragon. Dusk was upon us and the moon began to rise as the winter sun fell, creating a sunset that dreams are made of. As I was immersed in the beauty of the sky-scape, I noticed a spot appear, so high in the distance, becoming larger and larger. There was no mistaking this approaching reptilian silhouette, swooping down in ever-decreasing circles. Tan-y-Mynedd had arrived!

He landed in his usual ungainly fashion, within a cloud of shale and dust. His enormity appeared even greater as every muscle pumped with adrenaline. He shook his head, tail quivering, he began to speak. "I heard your call, Crach! We have never used the sacred whistle before, but at least we now know it works. Also, I need not ask you why I am here, I already know." His eyes glinted in the moonlight. "I am still searching for them, as I believe you have already heard."

"I have." My skin was tingling. "Carron told me. I sent him back to Ffestiniog to check all is as well as it can be at the moment."

"I think I know what has happened," he continued. "Dragon sensitivity is at the root of it. Even I was affected by the youngster's bloodlust. It makes your heart beat faster, and energy course through your limbs like a lightning strike. It is all most unsettling." His eyes rolled." There is little we dragons can do about it. Perhaps the closest thing humans can relate to is when they catch a chill. One gets it, so everybody in close vicinity will, as we were."

I found myself snuffling in reaction to the word 'chill'. Yes, indeed, the power of suggestion can be strong. Tan-y-Mynedd made his point most eloquently.

He continued, "Of course, if a chill is untreated, you can become delirious. A bloodlust is similar to that. Without the taste of blood, a madness overtakes the soul."

"Is there really no cure at all?" I asked.

He turned a huge head skywards, sighed, and replied, "No, Crach. Faerydae tried to keep him asleep, but, sadly, it did not work for long enough. He became very disruptive to the others, fighting and picking arguments, blind to all except one thing—blood. He is obsessed, Crach. Obsessed!" Tan-y-Mynedd sighed again. "This is going to end badly. Of that I am sure."

I felt he was right and shared the overwhelming sense of doom and despondency in the air.

We sat quietly, staring at a beautiful moon. It was chilly so I pulled the collar up around my neck for extra warmth. There was a biting breeze, with ice and snow in the sky. Suddenly, in the clarity of the night, a few snowflakes began to fall.

"Winter has arrived, Crach," Tan-y-Mynedd observed, looking up at the sky. "Snow will make it difficult for them to conceal themselves."

"And also, to find food," I added.

"Therein lies a problem, Crach. Remember the bloodlust?" His tail swished from side to side, a sign of anxiety in a dragon.

"You mean they will kill men?" I asked.

"I do, Crach. I do." He sighed again.

We sat together throughout the night far from the shelter of a cave, unable to sleep. We stayed as warm as was possible under the stars during such chilly hours. A fluttering of snow continued on and off, but it was not until dawn that it started to fall heavily, covering all under a massive white blanket. When the first shades of dawn crept into the sky, so did storm clouds, laden with more snow. Unable to see further than a few paces, I snuggled under Tan-y-Mynedd's wing, his armour protecting us both from freezing to death. I was blessed to have such a friend. Sill the snow fell, being late in the evening before it finally stopped. Tan-y-Mynedd shook himself violently, sending snow that had been covering him flying off in all directions. For a moment or two, I felt I was in the midst of yet another blizzard.

"The bird!" Tan-y-Mynedd exclaimed, pointing his head towards the sky. I followed his eyes and as sure as dragons are dragons and ravens are ravens, it was Carron flying swiftly towards us. He circled for a moment or two before landing on the great dragon's shoulder, which was a source of great relief to me. As you will remember, the raven's talons often connect with my shoulder! Tan-y-Mynedd had armour to protect his!

"Get off me, bird!" the dragon joked in protest.

"I am no mere 'bird', reptile! I am a raven, the most magical of birds!"

Would these two ever stop? This happened every time they met and yet they were the greatest of friends to each other as, of course, they were to me.

"I have urgent news!" squawked Carron. "The dragons have been seen attacking a village!"

"What?" Tan-y-Mynedd exclaimed in shock. "Where, Raven? Which village?"

"It is close to the Abbey at Cwmer. They have already killed two men, flying away with their bodies. Everybody saw it and there is no way any of this can be kept secret."

A tear came into Tan-y-Mynedd's huge eye, splashing to the ground. Our worst fears were now being realised. This was a crisis beyond any we could have envisaged.

"I am at a loss as to what we can do," I said, sadly recognising how hopeless this sounded.

Tan-y-Mynedd sighed so powerfully, snow puffed up in small clouds from the ground. "There is nothing we can do at the moment, Crach. The secret is out and although only one village has been attacked, it will spread like wildfire. The dragons will be hunted, Crach, and I know now I cannot save them. Nature must be allowed to take its course, if not, we are all doomed." He turned to Carron. "Fly to the Great Council of Blue Stone, bird. They must learn of what is happening."

As Carron flew off into the night, a great snowstorm rolled in from the north.

CHAPTER THIRTY-SEVEN

Three young dragons sat on a precipice overlooking the valley. Hunger making reptilian tummies rumble. They last ate three days ago, taking the dead men they killed from the village to a cave a few hundred paces from where they now sat. Young and inexperienced they may be, but they were rapidly becoming independent. Now with a taste and liking for the blood of man, there was no shortage of food to be had.

A carpet of snow covered the valley, the forest's green canopy was gone, buried under snowfall. Drifting snow made travel difficult, if not impossible, and villages were cut off and isolated. A bitterly cold wind gusted up the valley and the sky filled with yet more snow, ready to fall on the carpet of white below.

The dragons were restless, but not at all bothered by the

snow. Considering they had never seen freezing water before, they were not perplexed by it.

As the sky released further flurries of snow, the three dragons squawked to each other, flapped their wings, raised scaled heads, swished long tails and took off from the precipice, heading down into the valley beyond the forest. It was a spectacular sight to behold as they glided with their heads down and their eyes peeled, in search of prey.

On a small farm in the valley below, huddled in the harshness of winter, a man and boy forked hay for feeding their sheep who gathered in a corral by the side of a makeshift barn. As they worked, oblivious to the danger above, another boy came from the barn, and spotting the dragons in the sky, he screamed at his father and brother in abject terror.

One of the dragons swooped down and circled the barn, breathing fiercely gathering flame in his throat. Suddenly, another dragon dropped down, snatching the youth by the shoulders between sharp talons before sweeping back up again. The boy hung lifelessly in the air. The circling dragon expelled a huge breath of flame, stretching downwards with an intensity of heat igniting the barn in the flash of an eye. The frightened farmer screamed in horror on seeing the other dragon let go of his son and watched helplessly as he fell dead to the ground.

Now, the third dragon swooped down, landing with a crash in front of the farmer. Bending its head, it thrust a strong neck, snapping at the terrified man, only narrowly missing him with swords of sharp teeth. The farmer lunged in front of his son in an attempt to protect him, grabbing a pitchfork defensively as the dragon swung its head with jaws snapping. With pitchfork raised in front of him, he stabbed at the dragon, not seeing its fellow beast take his other son from behind. He was unaware until he heard screams of horror coming from above him.

The flames engulfing the barn now spread to the thatched roof of the farmhouse. Sparks took to flame and for a split second, the farmer caught sight of his burning home and dead sons, but that was all it took, one momentary lapse in concentration for the dragon to snap the man's head between its jaws. A headless, lifeless body fell to the ground as the dead farmer's life force gushed from his neck.

The three dragons began to feast on the corpses of the farmer and his sons laying on the blood-stained snow.

Nothing now remained of the farm, apart from ashes and the sound of wails from burning sheep. There was no longer any reminder of what had been there or of what had just occurred, as even the blood-stained snow disappeared when the heavens opened once more.

With full stomachs and appetites satisfied, the three dragons took flight, returning to their cave at the far end of the valley. It was time for them to sleep.

Chapter Thirty-Eight

Winter had well and truly arrived, bringing with it the beauty usual for the season. Glistening branches, laced with ice, and acres of white with hardly a blemish excepting for the tracks of animals, hunting for food, imprinted in the snow. I sat at the cave entrance, straining my eyes to see down the valley. I knew the young dragons had raided at least two homesteads and one village, but it had been quiet for a few days now. Tan-y-Mynedd brought me to the cave at my request, having declined his invitation to go to the Council of Blue Stone as I knew I was not needed there at the moment. Tan-y-Mynedd was more than capable of informing them of everything they needed to know, but they probably knew much already as would be expected at the occurrence of such a major event. He would give wise counsel to his elders, but

I did worry for his temper as, like me, he was exhausted by recent events. This past year had been the most difficult either of us had ever experienced in our entire lives. Well, this was certainly true for me anyway.

Trials and tribulations were the flavour of this last year and although Owain and the rebellion had enjoyed some success, the reality facing them right now was clear, they were hunted as outlaws and forced to hide in the forest in the midst of winter from the eyes of King Henry's men. This was not a situation Owain and I envisaged at the start of the year. All had happened so quickly.

My friends, Faerydae, Crow and Fwynedd, were exhausted from caring for the young dragons and we were all anxious beyond any understanding at the bloodlust which had developed in some of the youngsters.

The magical realms were quite upside down as centuries of history became unwittingly severed when Erasmus died and Henry witnessed the ravens leave the Tower. They now united with Carron, each taking a portion of our country to watch over whilst living independently of each other but, like the dragons, still connected through magic. Once facing extinction, dragons favoured anything but their demise, but now rogue dragons with bloodlust presented insurmountable problems, even the Council of Blue Stone would have no answers for.

I sat back and leaned against the cave wall, feeling the cold from the hard stone reach my skin through the tunic. I shuddered and tiredness overcame me, so I entered the cave to find my cot. Pulling thick sheepskins up around my chin, I closed my eyes and it was not long before sleep came. A dreamscape opened as I slumbered.

I found myself surrounded by swirling colours, immersed in a rainbow of light. I felt as if I was flying through the universe when suddenly, the rainbow was replaced by dark skies with thousands of stars flashing by at great speed. Now I felt I was falling helplessly downwards—down and down and down—as if there were no end. Still, I fell until it ended abruptly and I found myself sitting on a grassy knoll in beautiful sunlight, although the sky was purple and shimmering as if it may change colour at any moment. Even though I sat on this knoll, I had a sense of floating slightly above the ground. I felt a presence behind me and a familiar voice echoed across my dream.

"Hello, old friend," Llwyd ap Crachan Llwyd's voice filled my ears. "I disturb your sleep, for which I make no apology, Crach."

"There's none required," I replied, always pleased to see my old Master and to hear his wise counsel.

"This has been a hard year for you, Crach, and, in your mind, I think the most difficult ever."

He had done it again! Read my thoughts, but why break the habit of a lifetime in death?

"Why, indeed?" Once more, Llwyd ap Crachan Llwyd demonstrated his accurate hearing of 'my' thoughts.

"The winter is upon you and this year it will be particularly hard for everybody. The English are trying to cut off supplies to the rebels, but they will fail. As I told you before, the New Year will see an increase of a thousand-fold of those rushing to fight alongside their Prince. The English will suffer defeat in a great battle but there will be great sadness and confusion of betrayal or loyalty to the Welsh Crown."

"From what quarter?" I interjected, surprised by the extremes—betrayal or loyalty.

"Tudur will suggest the King's Pardon should be accepted." *He paused.*

"What 'Pardon'? There are no 'Pardons'," I asserted, knowing

what I said to be true.

"There will be, there will be," he shimmered in light, vibrating as he spoke.

"But why would Tudur want to accept a 'Pardon' from the usurper King? It goes against everything he believes?" I questioned, defending Tudur as I felt it was right for me to do.

"Crach, remember 'change is ever constant'. The brothers do not agree on everything, you know that." Llwyd ap Crachan Llwyd shimmered again. "Tudur is rapidly reaching his zenith as a warrior. He is tired, Crach, and, like the rest of you, running out of energy. You must help Tudur to make the correct decision, but, at all costs, attempt to maintain the love and loyalty between the two brothers. This will be a time of great pain, Crach. You will need my help, but know this." He paused. "You will be confronted with a crossroads and all will depend on your decision as to which road you take. Your wisdom will be the map on this journey."

All of this sounded to me as if I would rather avoid than confront such a scenario. I had known the Glyndwr brothers for many years, originally accompanying them on campaigns in Scotland. The first time I met Owain, we were young men. Me, a performing dwarf in a travelling circus and he, a student in law, studying at Lincolns Inn. That was back in 1375, twenty-six years ago, in the mists of time.

Llwyd ap Crachan Llwyd shimmered in his own aura as he spoke. "If only this was to be the sole problem you will have to face, Crach." He took a pause. "But it is not. Our dragon friends are united with the ravens and this is as it should be, now all links to our magical Kingdoms are severed with England and their usurper King. Whilst this gives us great strength, the recent slayings of men brought about by the bloodlust affecting three of the young dragons is a crisis, but you do not need me to remind you of that, but you do need me to tell you this. I see nothing but darkness, blood and death in their very short futures. Many more English will be slain by them and I see tongues wagging with tales of them being in league with the rebellion and that they are, indeed, the Prince's secret weapon."

"But that is just not true!" I interrupted my old Master.

"No, Crach, it is not, but that will not stop lies to seemingly have meaning towards truth. The dragons are frightening villagers and gossip of their atrocities is spreading as would a fire on summer bracken, from spark to flame in no time at all. Although I cannot see their imminent deaths, it is only a matter of time. As to when or how, I know not, but it is inevitable although that is not your problem. Tan-y-Mynedd has always wished the dragons to have no part in the rebellion which, of course, they have not, but these tales and rumours are feeding the fertile minds of the Welsh. Many are seeing the attacks on the English by the dragons as a good omen. The division this may cause is the problem you must address, Crach. Tan-y-Mynedd will need your friendship more than ever before."

"It seems as if I have no choice in these matters," I observed.

"None at all," came the reply.

"And the war?" I queried.

"It will go on, Crach, it will go on, but this next year, whilst all appears well posted in the heavens, there are dark clouds lurking in Owain's mind. Clouds bring movement, as you know, and your friendship will be challenged in ways you have never considered."

"So, you were not far wrong when you suggested this would be the hardest year of my life so far." I thought this past year was hard and the worst in my life, but now I have to be resigned to facing days yet to unfurl of pain and loss. I hope my resolve will help me to survive.

"It will, Crach!" he chuckled.

He had done it again!

As the shimmering form of Llwyd ap Crachan Llwyd faded. I had one thought in my mind.

"Justice will prevail!"

HISTORICAL NOTES
1375 - 1401

This book is the third in a series of novels introducing *'Crach Ffinnant'*, *magician, wizard, prophet and seer.* In reality, the story is total fantasy, but some of the characters did exist and some of the events are historically accurate but many are figments of my imagination. Obscure and lost in the mists of time, Crach Ffinnant is reborn from history as narrator of 'The Prophecy'.

'Crach Ffinnant' Very little is known about this fascinating man but his name appears in various historical text. R R Davies, in his narrative 'Owain Glyndwr Prince of Wales' (2009), describes Crach Ffinnant as 'prophet and seer' to Owain Glyndwr. 'Crach' means 'scab, scabby and, possibly, dwarf'. 'Ffinnant' would have been the name of his place of birth. Davies suggests that Crach Ffinnant would have been *'master of the rich heritage of legends and prophecies familiar to the Welsh people which rooted the miserable present into the glorious past and foresaw the day of the return of such glories.'* It is said that, in the same way politicians today have their 'spin doctors' to interpret the signs of the times, so Welsh leaders of the period had their 'seers' and Owain Glyndwr had Crach Ffinnant. We know they were acquainted as far back as 1384 as Crach accompanied Owain Glyndwr and his brother, Tudur Glyndwr, during their military service under

Sir Gregory Sais to Berwick on Tweed. Crach Ffinnant was at Owain Glyndwr's side on the 16 September 1400 when his Lord was proclaimed 'Prince of Wales'.

'**Owain Glyndwr Prince of Wales**' said to be the only true Prince of Wales, he was a direct descendant of the Royal Line of the Princes of Powys. He was born sometime between the years of 1335–1359, disappearing from history around 1415. After his father, Gruffyd Fychan, died, Owain, still under age, became a Royal Ward. In 1375 the young Glyndwr studied law at Lincoln's Inn, sent by his appointed guardian, Sir David Hanmer, which is not surprising as he himself was a lawyer, Kings Serjeant and legal advisor to Richard II. In 1383 Glyndwr married Sir David Hanmer's daughter, Margaret, and together they had five sons and four or five daughters. He began his military experiences the next year, in 1384, along with his brother, Tudur, fighting in Scotland and Ireland under the banners of King Richard II. In 1397, possibly by seeing the gradual demise of Richard II, who was essentially by now King in name only, Glyndwr had no choice but to switch sides to Henry Bollingsbroke, who would later become King Henry IV.

'**Tudur Glyndwr**' Brother to Owain Glyndwr.

'**Margaret Glyndwr**' Wife to Owain Glyndwr and daughter of Sir David Hanmer.

'**Iolo Goch**' (1320-1398) was a highly trained professional bard whose long career spanned a period of profound social change in Wales. He was a frequent visitor to Sycharth, the home of Owain Glyndwr, and records life as it was in his poetry, some of which still survives today. In his work 'Praise of Owain Glyndwr', he alludes to magic and prophecy and also to the good and generous nature, abilities and intellect of Glyndwr. He may have had a brother but Master Healan (as he was known in his role as Apothecary in London but returning to his true name of Myrddin Goch ap Cwnwrig upon his return to his homeland of Wales) was not he, that is my fantasy.

'**Lincoln's Inn**' can still be found in London today and has been training Barristers at Law since 1310. Owain Glyndwr studied law there in 1375.

'**Richard II**' *was Plantagenet king of England from 1377 to 1399 and was usurped by Henry IV.* In September 1398, a quarrel between two former appellants, Gaunt's son Henry Bolingbroke and Thomas Mowbray, Duke of Norfolk, gave the king another opportunity for revenge and he banished them both. When Gaunt died in February 1399, Richard confiscated the vast Lancastrian estates, which would have passed to Bolingbroke. In May, Richard left to campaign in Ireland. Bolingbroke invaded England and rallied both noble and popular support. Returning to England in August, Richard surrendered without a fight. In September, he abdicated and Bolingbroke ascended the throne as Henry IV. In October, Richard was imprisoned in Pontefract Castle, where he died four months later.

'**Henry IV**' *The first of three monarchs from the house of Lancaster, Henry usurped the crown and successfully consolidated his power despite repeated uprisings.* Richard surrendered in August and Henry was crowned in October 1399, claiming that Richard had abdicated of his own free will. Henry's first task was to consolidate his position. Most rebellions were quashed easily, but the revolt of the Welsh Squire Owain Glyndwr in 1400 was more serious.

'**Bishop of St Asaph**' **John Trevor** (Welsh Ieuan Trefor) (died 10 April 1410), or John Trevaur, was Bishop of St Asaph in Wales. He was provided to the see of St Asaph on 21

October 1394. His original name was Ieuan, which he later anglicised to John and took on the surname Trevor. Trevor's brother Adda was married to the sister of Owain Glyndwr who appointed him as an ambassador to the French court.

'Lord Henry Percy 'Hotspur' was born 20 May 1364 in Northumberland the eldest son of <u>Henry Percy, 1st Earl of Northumberland</u>. Percy's military and diplomatic service brought him substantial marks of royal favour in the form of grants and appointments but despite this, the Percy family decided to support Henry Bolingbroke, the future Henry IV. Under the new king, Percy had extensive civil and military responsibility in both the east march towards Scotland and in north Wales, where he was appointed High Sheriff of Flintshire in 1399. In north Wales, he was under increasing pressure as a result of the Welsh rebellion and in March 1402, Henry IV appointed Percy royal lieutenant in north Wales.

'Rhys ap Tudur' was a <u>Welsh</u> nobleman and a member of the <u>Tudor family of Penmynydd</u>. He held positions of power on behalf of King <u>Richard II of England</u>, including two periods as the <u>Sheriff of Anglesey</u> in the 1370s and 80s. Rhys accompanied the king on a military expedition to Ireland in 1398, but in 1400 began to support the revolt of his cousin <u>Owain Glynd⬚r</u> against King <u>Henry IV of England</u>. In 1401, he and his brother <u>Gwilym ap Tudur</u> took <u>Conway Castle</u> after infiltrating it.

'Sycharth' sits in the valley of the river Cynllaith, a tributary of the <u>Afon Tanat</u>. The site of <u>Owain Glynd⬚r</u>'s castle lies about a kilometre to the west of the boundary between England and Wales with a belt of woodland on the higher ground to the east known as Parc Sycharth.

'Valle Crucis Abbey' (Valley of the Cross) is a <u>Cistercian</u> abbey located in <u>Llantysilio</u> in <u>Denbighshire</u>, <u>Wales</u>. More formally *the Abbey Church of the Blessed Virgin Mary, Valle Crucis* it is known in Welsh both as *Abaty Glyn Egwestl* and *Abaty Glyn y Groes*. The abbey was built in 1201 by Madog ap Gruffydd Maelor, Prince of Powys Fadog. The abbey is believed to have housed up to sixty brethren, 20 choir monks and 40 lay-members who would have carried out the day-to-day duties, including agricultural work. The abbey is believed to have been involved in the Welsh Wars of Edward I of England during the 13th century, and was damaged in the uprising led by Owain Glynd⊠r.

'Pillar of Eliseg' Known as *Elise's Pillar* or *Croes Elisedd* in Welsh it stands near Valle Crucis Abbey. It was erected by Cyngen ap Cadell (died 855), King of Powys in honour of his great-grandfather Elisedd ap Gwylog.

'Triduum' The period of three days that begins with the liturgy on the evening of Maundy Thursday, reaches its high point in the Easter Vigil, and closes with evening prayer on Easter Sunday.

Pronunciation Of Welsh Names In Ravens And Dragons Phonetic Guide

Crach Ffinnant: kraach (as in loch) Fin-ant

Tan y Mynedd: Tan er mun-eeth

Owain Glyndwr: Oh-wine Glin-doo-hr ('rh' sounds like an escape of air)

Llwyd ap Crachan Llwyd: (LL = smile and put your tongue on the back of your teeth to make a list sound_ Thlooeed app kraach-ann Thloeed

Rhys ap Tudur: hrees app ti-deer

Fwynedd: Vooi-neth (th as in this)

Conwy: Con-ooee (rhymes with puy)

Sycharth: Such (as in lock) - arth

Llangollen: thlan-go (as in gone)- thlen

CRACH FFINNANT
JUSTICE WILL PREVAIL

VOLUME IV

CHAPTER ONE

Reginald de Grey sat on his horse, feeling somewhat pleased with himself. Wales was now crawling with troops of English soldiers, searching for Glyndwr and his rebels. Glyndwr was now an outlaw, with all his lands forfeited. To say he felt smug is somewhat of an understatement. With his usual arrogance now raised several notches, he was unbearable.

Meetings at Ruthin with Hotspur had been a little frustrating, to say the least. Henry Percy did not like Reginald de Grey as it was he who had been responsible for creating even more serious problems with The Crown for Glyndwr. Reginald de Grey was in dispute with the Prince over ownership of Glyndwr's boundaries and land and at a Royal Court, Richard II found in Owain's favour. When King Richard was usurped and imprisoned by Henry, Reginald de Grey was given Royal Command to seize Glyndwr's lands. Henry gave instructions to Reginald de Grey, ordering him to tell Glyndwr to attend him in Scotland where he was attempting a campaign. By the time Reginald de Grey condescended to inform Glyndwr, it was too late to respond, even if he had wanted to. Henry branded Glyndwr a traitor and Reginald de Grey was jubilant. Hotspur had much respect for Glyndwr, acknowledging he was a gentleman and a warrior. He recognised Reginald de Grey was neither of these things, despite his outward demeanour.

Twenty men rode with Reginald de Grey. He was riding

at the head of the procession, perched on his mount like a preening peacock. A cold wind blew from the north and flurries of snow created drifts here and there. The riders had their collars pulled up to try and keep warm and some wore sacks over their shoulders for extra protection, although Reginald De Grey sported a bear skin over his! They had gone but a few leagues from Ruthin when fallen snow-laden trees blocked their path. As snow became deeper, the horses stumbled and refused any attempt to negotiate their way over the fallen trees.

"Sergeant at Arms!" Reginald de Grey hailed the soldier in charge of the small troop. "Get this moved, we must make haste!"

Looking at his men, The Sergeant at Arms shrugged his shoulders whilst averting his eyes skywards, silently waving to his men for assistance. Four dismounted and began to tie ropes to a tree, then connected the rope to the pommel of their saddles with the intention of dragging the trees off the path. Others dismounted, seizing the opportunity to get out of the saddle and stamp their feet in an attempt to move freezing blood into freezing limbs.

"Come along, no slacking. Get a move on or we will all freeze to death!" Reginald de Grey pulled his bearskin tightly around himself. "By the Gods, I am perished to the bone."

"How the hell does he think we feel?" Whispered one soldier to another.

"He don't care." Came a quiet reply.

Riders urged their horses forward and the rope grew taut, stretching and creaking as the fallen tree began to slide a little.

"Ah, good!" Exclaimed Reginald de Grey. "It moves." Unfortunately, his horse was not used to seeing trees travel along the ground, hence it began to prance. "Stand still!" He

.

screamed, digging spurs into his horse's side in frustration. At this, his mount reared and slipped, sending Reginald de Grey tumbling to the ground, landing in an unceremonious heap, sinking into the soft snow. He was livid! His temper got worse when every time he tried to stand up, down he would slip again. Not a straight face could be seen amongst the soldiers as each and every one were beside themselves with hysteria. Never had there been a funnier sight in a very long time. The Sergeant at Arms held his sides, trying to prevent them from splitting. Others slapped knees and backs and the more each laughed, the more others did too. Reginald de Grey was now in a real rage. "Help me, you churls!" But down he slipped again, and the laughter grew louder!

Thomas Clements, a twenty-one year old from London, shivered and his eyes suddenly became lifeless as an arrow struck him in the throat. He fell dead to the ground.

"Holy sh...." The Sergeant at Arms was unable to finish his words as he rapidly became the second to fall as two arrows hit him square in the chest. Two soldiers fell from their horses as others tried to defend themselves against an unseen enemy, concealed in the shadows. A hail of arrows flew through the air and five more soldiers dropped into the snow.

"Enough! We surrender!" One of the soldiers shouted as he threw his arms in to the air in resignation of capture, believing it a better alternative to death. All the others quickly followed, tossing their weapons into the snow. They looked around in the silence that followed as forty Welsh rebels stepped out of the shadows of the trees and surrounded them, bows loaded and pulled, swords drawn.

"On your knees!" Ordered Thomas Fychan, a blacksmith from Powys.

They all fell to their knees, whilst Reginald de Grey, now

on his feet, looked around at his captors with fear in his eyes but still with arrogance on his lips. "What are you doing? Are you deranged? Do you not know who I am?"

Two of the rebels bowed, sarcastically. "Oh, yes, my Lord. Indeed, we do!" Said one.

"You are our prisoner!" Said another.

"And, who are you, Sir, that you assault a Knight of the Realm who holds the King's favours?"

"Fine words for a pig!" Thomas Fychan grabbed Reginald de Grey by the shoulders and threw him down into the snow. "On your knees, you were told! Stay down there or I will cut your throat so deep that your head will come right off!" He laughed at his own joke.

"Come, Thomas, let him be! Bind the peacock!" Emrys appeared from the trees. "Baron de Grey, you are my prisoner and thus your life, or your death, is now at the will of our Prince, Owain Glyndwr.

De Grey went pale when he heard Glyndwr's name and began to tremble from head to toe.

Emrys pressed home his point. "You will be confined at Glyndwr's pleasure."

"What?" De Grey protested.

Emrys turned on him quickly. "You are to be ransomed, Sir. Your weight in gold, or you die!"

If it was at all possible to turn any paler than he was already, he did. In fact, his pallor matched the snow he kneeled upon."

"Bind him to his horse!" Emrys ordered. Two of the rebels bound Reginald de Grey to his steed, but not before removing fancy rings from his fingers and the gold chain from around his neck. "You won't be needing these!" One of the rebels announced.

"Alyn! Give me those, they are for the Prince." Emrys grabbed the rings and chain, and thrust the gold jewellery into the saddle bag on his horse.

The English soldiers and Reginald de Grey looked a sorry sight, bound to their horses, fear etched on pale faces as the procession led by Emrys moved off in single file through the snow.

Flurries of snow soon turned into a full-blown blizzard. The riders bent their heads into the wind in an attempt to prevent the freezing snow blinding them. Beards and hair exposed to the elements, froze white with ice. Noses turned purple with cold, while fingers and feet became numb.

De Grey recognised that any attempt at escape was futile as the rebels would surely prefer to kill him anyway. His decision was to do nothing but keep his head down. This was, indeed, the most sensible action under the circumstances.

The procession of rebels and captors rode on as the blizzard reduced in severity, enabling visibility to improve a little. Now they could at least see the rider in front of them.

Emrys halted his men. "We will make camp for the night here at the edge of the forest, boys!" Emrys dismounted and passed the reins of his horse to another soldier. "Get a fire going and let's have some food." He told them. "And tie the prisoners to each other, except for Reginald de Grey. He will be isolated from the rest."

Of course, Reginald de Grey protested at his treatment, being manhandled and verbally abused, but Emrys reminded him that a sharp knife would soon stop his moaning. De Grey became silent and morose, not at all his usual arrogant self. Sitting alone isolated from the others with his back against a tree, closing tired eyes, trying to block out the catastrophe he found himself to be in, he prayed for sleep to come, but it would not. Instead voices of rebels, speaking in Welsh, a language he did not understand, echoed in his ears, he knew not what they were talking about. Paranoid thoughts began to enter his mind. *'What if the rebels killed him before they arrived at Glyndwr's camp? What if he were to reach there, and Glyndwr decided to kill him? There was no love lost between the two and he was, after all, responsible for Glyndwr's problems with the King in the first place. What if Henry refused to pay the ransom?'* He had so many questions and all were without answers. Once again, he tried to sleep, without success.

The night came and with it, a further drop in temperature. Emrys and his men huddled around a fire, blazing in the dark, causing shadows to dance amongst the trees. Lookouts were relieved by others and came to sit at the fire to thaw themselves out. Emrys decided to allow the prisoners and Reginald de Grey to come closer to the blaze. He did not think Owain would be too pleased with him if he let them all freeze to death.

In the morning, as dawn broke on the horizon, the rebels stamped the fire out, burying the embers in an attempt to conceal any evidence of their camp. The prisoners were cajoled and bundled onto their horses and re-tied. Reginald de Grey once again protested at the treatment he was receiving so Emrys reminded him of what would happen if he were not quiet, waving a knife menacingly under his nose to emphasis his point.

Emrys took hold of the pommel of the saddle and hauled himself up onto his horse. He turned in the saddle and lifting his arm, waved to his men. All silently moved into the forest. Reginald de Grey looked around to see if there was anything of note, but all that met his eyes were trees, hundreds of them.

The procession rode on through the forest in silence for at

least half a day before entering a clearing. They had arrived at the rebels' encampment. Reginald de Grey saw the rebels were well organised. They had built huts and stables in a semi-circle which housed Glyndwr's army and their horses. A communal kitchen sat on the other side, pots hung over fires where some men stirred pans with wooden spoons, whilst others sliced up venison for the meal. At the far side of the compound was a blacksmiths' barn, alive with the hammering of hot iron. Amongst sparks that flew here and there, were two large Welshmen, working at anvils, covered in sweat.

Rows of mountain ponies were tethered to long ropes, heads deep in nosebags, enjoying grain. With thick coats they were content in the winter cold.

Emrys dragged Reginald de Grey from his horse and holding him by the shoulders, said. "And now, my fine feathered peacock, time for you to face justice!" He pushed him towards the largest of the buildings. "Move!"

Owain Glyndwr stood on the veranda. He quietly waited, watching Emrys shove and push Reginald de Grey through the snow towards him. The fine Lord was not looking his usual preened and arrogant self - indeed, just the opposite.

I stood next to Owain and although he rarely flew into a temper, I could sense he was seething at the sight of Reginald de Grey.

"Well, my Prince, here he is, at last!" I said.

Owain did not answer immediately, he was glaring at Reginald de Grey, tapping irritated fingers on the hilt of his dagger which hung at a waist belt. My Prince then replied quietly, as if trying to contain anger bubbling under the surface. "It is him. I have a mind to forget all about a ransom!"

"My Lord!" Emrys bowed his head and pushed Reginald de Grey to his knees in front of us. "This is Baron de Grey of

Ruthin." He paused. "An old friend?" He asked, sarcastically.

"So, what will I do with you, Baron? Cut your throat? Bury you in a tree alive? I have so many options." Owain stepped towards the Baron and fetched him a hard slap with the back of his hand, full in the face. De Grey was knocked from his knees at the force of the slap. His nose bled and a cut opened on his lip.

"Right, that made me feel a bit better, Crach!" He smiled a little for the first time since the Baron arrived at our compound. "I have no more words for this man at the moment. Emrys, chain him in the stables. Give him some food to keep him alive." Owain lifted a hand to strike Reginald de Grey once more, but left it hovering in the air as Emrys dragged him to his feet, kicked his backside and pushed the Baron in the direction of the stables.

"So, Crach." Owain put his arm around my shoulders as we turned around to go back into the warmth of the hut. "Time to send a letter to Henry. Let's see if he will give gold for Baron de Grey. Or maybe he would rather have his head?"